IN A STRANGER'S EYES

IN A STRANGER'S EYES

Rebekah Ross

TATE PUBLISHING & *Enterprises*

In a Stranger's Eyes
Copyright © 2011 by Rebekah Ross. All rights reserved.

No part of this publication may be reproduced, stored in a retrieval system or transmitted in any way by any means, electronic, mechanical, photocopy, recording or otherwise without the prior permission of the author except as provided by USA copyright law.

This novel is a work of fiction. Names, descriptions, entities, and incidents included in the story are products of the author's imagination. Any resemblance to actual persons, events, and entities is entirely coincidental.

The opinions expressed by the author are not necessarily those of Tate Publishing, LLC.

Published by Tate Publishing & Enterprises, LLC
127 E. Trade Center Terrace | Mustang, Oklahoma 73064 USA
1.888.361.9473 | www.tatepublishing.com

Tate Publishing is committed to excellence in the publishing industry. The company reflects the philosophy established by the founders, based on Psalm 68:11,
"The Lord gave the word and great was the company of those who published it."

Book design copyright © 2011 by Tate Publishing, LLC. All rights reserved.
Cover design by Blake Brasor
Interior design by Lindsay B. Behrens

Published in the United States of America
ISBN: 978-1-61739-686-1
1. Fiction / General   2. Fiction / Suspense
11.03.29

DEDICATION

To my best friend Keith Ramsour who passed away in January 2010. He was always there for me when I was ready to put my pencil down. He always encouraged me never to give up.

To Benita:
A wonderful woman that I'm so blessed to meet!

Rebekah Ross

ACKNOWLEDGMENTS

Writing this novel took me nearly three years to complete—being a single mother of three teenagers, working two jobs, and going to college. I feel as if this is one of my many accomplishments I have successfully done. I would like to thank my kids, Sam, Katlyn, and Hannah for being supportive when I worked several hours taking time away from them. Also, my sisters, Rita and Cheryl, for being there to help me and my kids when we needed them for anything. They were always there. I have such great support from all of my family. I would also like to thank my Grandma Ross, who has always been my rock, as well as my mother.

CHAPTER 1

The birds were chirping outside as Katie rolled over to turn off her alarm clock. Adjusting her eyes to her new house every morning was always surreal to her. Lying back down in her king-size bed for a few more minutes, Katie enjoyed the peace and quiet she longed so many years for. A petite woman at age forty-five, she would hold many titles.

A single mother of three children who were following their dreams, but not without a price, learning lessons throughout life dealing with peer pressure and drugs. Now all in their twenties, Katie was amazed at how their lives would change in so many directions throughout the years. Jacob, now twenty-eight, suffered many mental illnesses growing up. Now working as a back-up dancer for a well-known pop star touring the country, he longed to stay sober for other teens. Devon, now twenty-six, lived and worked in California as a choreographer for many celebrities. Ashley, her youngest, and a spitting image of her mother, would become grew up to follow in her Mom's footsteps and became a Corrections Officer and Model.

Katie, having worked in law enforcement for fifteen years, watched people cross her path that would send chills down her spine. A person with a strong personality, Katie would always be the person that would always try to make a situation better with a smile. Dealing with troubled adults on a daily basis, Katie learned how life on the inside really was. An army brat for most of her childhood until her teens, Katie had respect for anyone she came in contact with. Raised in a middle-class neighborhood in St. Louis, Katie learned at a young age that no matter the color of a person, everyone was made the same, inside and out. Being raised around the military and being bussed to an all-black school in the '80s, Katie learned that as a group formed to better our society as a whole.

Getting ready for her morning jog, Katie stopped by her dresser to put up her long brown hair. Smiling, she grabbed her iPod and cell phone and headed downstairs. A woman now owning and running two businesses from her house, Katie never took for granted anything she was blessed with. An author of several books, Katie hired her two sisters to run her library on the upper level of her house. With her book factory nearly an hour away, Katie left her mother in charge of everything there. Her second business, which Katie started from a small business to a huge profession, a model since her early twenties, Katie loved her photography business just as much. Another passion since a young child, Katie turned her hobby as a photographer into a profession, adding more to her portfolio as a model. Her dream house was built on twelve hundred acres. Katie had her own private jet, along with her pilot living with his wife and daughter in the guesthouse. Also having houses built for her sisters, mother and stepfather, father and stepmom, Katie loved the fact her family was so close. With both businesses bringing in millions of dollars every year, Katie still longed for the simple things in life. Walking down the spiral stairs to the main floor, Katie looked at her living room full of pictures of her family.

Checking the time on her cell phone, Katie realized her daydreaming was cutting in to her time to enjoy the beautiful country. *Six in the morning already*, she thought to herself, knowing her sisters would be arriving within the hour. With Mark, her pilot, flying to Kentucky to pick up her seven models for the day, Katie was grateful her vacation was only four days away. Katie looked forward to going to Florida for a week at her beach house. Working every day for the past six months, Katie longed for a much-needed break. Stopping by the refrigerator for a water bottle, Katie began her daily stretch and headed out the backdoor. Not realizing the door shut so hard, Katie stopped and felt as if her life was spinning in circles. Sweaty, Katie saw a man's face in his late thirties; a man that would rape several women before getting caught, leaving the women and their families to pick up the pieces. Knowing she had daughters as well, Katie always prayed something like that wouldn't happen to them.

Beep! Beep!

Katie snapped out of her trance.

"Katie, I'm leaving Kentucky. I'll be there in a little while; just a heads up," Mark said.

"Thanks," Katie said, knowing her time to jog was not an option today. Dealing with scary flashbacks for nearly a year, Katie sought help through many doctors. From dealing with sexual abuse from someone close to her as a child until what she thought would be a man she would spend her life with, Katie, then in her thirties, would walk away from the abuse and take her three children with her. Moving past that was one of the hardest things to deal with.

The second oldest of four daughters, Katie was to remain one of the middle children until age nineteen, when her sister Marcy passed away due to heart failure at age twenty, leaving two children behind. Marcy, having nothing but chaos her whole life—from dealing with sexual, mental, and physical abuse in the house to giving birth to her son in a group home at age fifteen—Marcy never seemed to enjoy a normal life. What seemed normal as an adult, Katie wished Marcy could come back to her family and enjoy all the good things life had to offer.

Going back upstairs to get ready for her day, Katie heard her two sisters come in the front door for work.

"Hey, sis. I'll make breakfast," Rachel said, knowing she didn't have time to eat, getting her kids ready for school.

"Okay, thanks. Casey, will you run downstairs and turn on all my equipment before Mark gets here with the models?" Katie asked, grateful they always worked together as a team.

"Sure thing, sis. Meet us in the kitchen, please, so we can have our meeting before our vacation starts next week," Casey said, knowing Katie was still pale from her flashback.

"Hey, Katie, real quick. Are you okay?" Casey asked, worried.

"Yes, I'm still dealing with that problem; I just wish they would go away," Katie said. "I'll meet you in a few minutes!"

Fearing her bad flashbacks would always haunt her, Katie went to her bathroom to splash cold water on her face, then picked out an outfit for the day. Throwing some makeup on, Katie got dressed and headed downstairs to eat some breakfast. *Beep! Beep!* she went to grab her phone out of her purse.

"Yeah, Mark," she said, feeling better already.

"We just landed. We will be there in twenty minutes. Okay, boss?" Mark said, knowing he would put a smile on her face.

"Thanks, see you in a bit," she said, hoping Rachel had the food ready.

"Hey, you look better!" Rachel said, smiling.

Casey walked back up the stairs from the studio. "You're ready to go, sis!" Casey said.

"Thanks for everything this morning. Vacation starts in a few days; are you ladies doing anything exciting?" Katie asked, knowing they were all running out of time.

With teenagers of their own, Katie knew the more time Rachel and Casey made for their kids, the better.

"Yes, today is Thursday. Technically, we have today and Friday because you're off work Saturday and Sunday, unless you have some last minute things to do," Katie said, knowing she had to leave the book factory running as usual.

"Mom is taking vacation too, right?" Casey asked.

"Yes, it will be fine. The supervisors will be there, and my phone will be on too," Katie said, hearing a truck pull up with Mark and the models. "I'll catch up with you this afternoon; my day should end by four o'clock. Thanks for everything this morning."

She went to greet her models. A system Katie set up herself, she would start a Web site and choose only professional models to fly to her studio. Charging a flat rate of five hundred dollars each, Katie hired a chef to come in Monday through Friday to fix all their meals. With airfare, hair, makeup and wardrobe included, Katie took pride in how she set up her studio with an in-ground pool and an adult playroom. Katie also had her darkroom set up to give them their proofs, comp cards, and a CD for future reference. With seven models scheduled from different states within range of each other, she had all her models lined up for months in advance. Working in the modeling field for over twenty years, Katie was able to do their hair, makeup, and wardrobe at no extra cost to them. Kicking her day into high gear, Katie started her daily tour by showing her models exactly how their day would go.

With a personality to fit everyone else's, Katie was truly blessed to help so many people. Working in law enforcement so many years, Katie couldn't believe most things her eyes would see. From working around inmates daily, Katie could shake her head at people that would make the worst choices and leave their families to pick up the pieces. Trying to gather their mentality most of the time, Katie would hold her head up high and pray for a safer world. With her day flying by, Katie heard Sheri upstairs getting lunch prepared.

"Lunchtime!" Katie said as she followed them all upstairs. Sheri, a single mother like Katie, would count her blessings every day for Katie and her kids. Meeting them at a restaurant one night, Katie could see how much she struggled, and knowing she could prepare any kinds of meals, Katie hired her to make up menus from all across the globe.

"Mexican today, Ms. Katie!" Sheri said, smiling.

"That smells great; we are all starving, I'm sure," Katie said, knowing she would eat with everyone else. With the excitement still in the air, Katie gathered everyone back downstairs to finish up their day. Turning the music on, Katie knew the rest of her day would fly, as always. *Beep! Beep!* she heard from her desk.

"Hey, Mark. We are almost done for the day," Katie said, always trying to keep him up-to-date.

"Okay, boss. I'll see you in thirty minutes," he said.

Beep! Beep!

Thinking it was Mark again, she saw Ashley's name come up on her phone.

"Hey, honey. I'm finishing up in the studio; I'll call you back in a little while, okay?" Katie said, knowing Ashley related to her hectic schedule, modeling herself.

She just said, "Okay. Love you. Bye."

Finishing up in her darkroom, Katie heard Mark come in the backdoor. "Okay, everyone. Great job today; I hope you all had a good time!" Katie said, following them upstairs to meet her pilot. Thanking Sheri for all her hard work, Katie walked back downstairs to call Ashley back and clean her studio for the next day. "Hey, sweetie!" Katie said to her daughter, always happy to hear her voice.

"Hey, Mom. Are you going to be home tonight?" Ashley said.

"Yes. Are you coming over?" Katie said, turning some of her music on to get in the mood to clean.

"Yeah, but do you want to meet me in town for Chinese, then go back to your house and swim?" Ashley said, knowing it was time for some mother-daughter time.

"Sure. What time is good for you?" Katie said, already excited.

"I have to run home and change after work and grab my swimsuit for your house," Ashley said, knowing her twelve-hour days at the jail were getting to her.

"So, seven at Green China?" her mom asked.

"Sure. See you there. Love you. Bye!" Ashley said.

Rarely getting out, Katie was excited about meeting her daughter. She lived only three miles away, but they still had trouble seeing each other.

"Hey, Katie!" she heard from the top of the spiral stairs.

"Yeah, come on down, please!" Katie said.

"We are done for the day; we just wanted to come down and tell you to have a good night," Casey said.

"Thanks for everything; I would be lost without you!" Katie told them, hurrying to finish the studio.

"Got a date?" Rachel asked, smiling.

"Actually, yes. Ashley called, and we are going to dinner. Do you want to join us?" Katie said, not wanting to leave them out.

"No, we have to meet our husbands and kids here in a little bit, but thanks," Rachel said.

"Okay, I'm going to try to jog before dinner; I was distracted this morning," Katie said, knowing her sisters were one of the few people that new about her problem.

"Katie, I hope things get better; it worries me every day. You should tell your kids," Casey said.

"No, they have enough to worry about, and the doctor said it could just be temporary," Katie said, turning the lights off in her studio and heading upstairs to thank her chef.

"Okay, we don't want something bad to happen to you and then have to try to explain it to your kids when you are gone," Rachel said, hoping she would give in.

"I will be fine; go home to your families. I love you, and thanks for everything," Katie said, smiling, giving them both a hug good-bye and watched them head back out the front door.

"Hey, Sheri. How are you?" Katie asked her chef.

Sheri, a woman in her early 50's, stood only 4'11 and always struggled to get where she was in life day by day. A small woman with black hair and brown eyes, Sheri had come over from Mexico and became a United States citizen, marrying the man she was in love with for many years. After she had found out from a string of several women that he was cheating on her, Sheri had taken her two small children at the time and moved to Missouri where her family resided. Learning the hard way, as most of us do, Sheri refused to be with a man she couldn't trust. A past with a lot of regret turned her life around, meeting Katie a few times at a restaurant near Katie's studio, then in town. Finding out they had a lot more in common, the women had formed a bond nobody could break.

"Good. No work next week, right?" Sheri said.

"Yes, paid vacation for you!" Katie told her.

"Thanks, and have fun in Florida!" Sheri said. "I have leftovers from lunch; I'll leave them for you, if you get hungry later."

"Thanks, but Ashley and I are going to dinner!" Katie said.

"Have fun; you deserve it!" Sheri said, packing up her things and leaving out the backdoor.

As Katie headed upstairs to get ready for a late jog before meeting Ashley, she grabbed her phone to check her voice mail. Katie was shocked to hear a familiar man's voice.

"Hey, Katie. It's Caleb. I was moving and found your number. I just called to see how you were doing," he said, sounding as if he didn't age at all.

Wow! she thought to herself as she put her phone down to get ready for her jog. Caleb, an army man going through a divorce back then, was on the rebound when he met her through her best friend, Cammie. For the first time since she left Mike, Caleb would give her butterflies, but it would be the day that his other girlfriend would call her out of the blue and tell Katie exactly how he was. Not believing the woman on the phone, Katie had decided to find out on her own and drive to his house many states away before realizing he was exactly how the woman said he was. Shaking her head, shocked to hear his voice, Katie deleted the message and went to get ready for her dinner with Ashley. Confident, Katie knew someday she would meet a man that was truly going to treat her the way she deserved to be treated.

Grabbing her purse, Katie headed downstairs to meet Ashley. She went to the garage and drove her BMW to town. With the weather in the seventies, Katie decided to put the top down on her convertible and enjoy her freedom—something she never thought would be so sacred. With her finances taken care of, Katie had no worries, except the common ones as a mother. Pulling up to the restaurant, Katie saw Ashley's Jeep and ran over to give her a hug.

A grown woman now, Katie couldn't believe she would be so tall. Heading inside, Ashley said, "Mom, before we go in, I want to tell you something."

"What?" Katie asked, scared something was terribly wrong.

"I'm resigning the jail and moving to Hollywood to further my modeling and acting career," Ashley said, knowing her mom loved her working there. Katie, relieved she wasn't going to be a grandmother yet, hugged her and told her she would support her in her decision to leave after only being there a year.

Eating dinner, Katie and Ashley caught up on each other's lives. Talking on the phone is never the same as having great company. Katie thought to herself as they ate, and then they headed back to Katie's house to go swimming.

Getting into her car, Katie checked her phone for any new messages. *Four missed calls,* she thought to herself. Listening to her voice mail, she was happy Jacob and Devon called close to the same time, both from different states. Knowing the other two had to be business-related, Katie called her kids back first.

"Hello, Devon," Katie said.

"Hey, Mom. I haven't talked to you in a couple of weeks. I just wanted to see how you were doing before you headed to Florida," Devon said.

"Thanks. I'm doing well; I just met Ashley for dinner in town. Now we are heading to my house to go swimming," Katie told her, wishing she were closer and not so busy.

"I wish I could be there to hang out too; I miss all of you!" Devon said.

"I miss you too. You should come stay with me a couple of days at the beach house; it will be a lot of fun," Katie said.

"Actually, Mom, I will work hard to come to see you," Devon said. "I have missed you terribly!"

"Okay. Thanks for calling, sweetie; you made my day better," she said, missing her being able to just stop by.

"No problem, Mom. I love you and miss you. Bye for now," Devon said, hanging up her phone.

"Love you too. Bye," Katie said. *Wow, I should buy a lottery ticket,* she thought, amazed that all three of her kids called on the same day.

Calling Jacob back, Katie was caught off guard by a different voice answering his phone. "Hello. Is Jacob there?" Katie said, shocked to hear a woman's voice.

"Yes, you must be his mother," she said.

"Yes, is he around?" Katie asked.

"Hey, Mom. How have you been?" he said.

"I'm good, but you sound better," Katie said, laughing. "New girlfriend?"

"Yes, we have been dating a couple of weeks," Jacob said, knowing she would be happy for him.

"Is she a dancer too?" Katie asked curiously.

"Yes, she travels with us. Her name is Christy," Jacob said.

"I'm happy for you both; I can't wait to meet her. Are you coming home to visit any time soon?" Katie asked, pulling into her driveway.

"Yes, we will be in Missouri next month. I'll call you before then, though. I love you, Mom," he said.

"I love you too. Thanks for calling; I've heard from all three of you kids in the same day," Katie said, saying her good-byes to her son. With Ashley getting out of her Jeep, waiting for her mom to get off the phone, Katie told her how she talked to Devon and Jacob on her way home.

"How are they doing?" Ashley asked, heading to the bathroom to change. "I'm going upstairs to change and check my other messages," she said, walking to her room.

Shutting the door behind her, Katie stopped in her tracks, getting dizzy. She sat down on her bed. With no distractions, she saw a young child's face. Abducted in the middle of the night from her bed, the little girl—only four years old—would never be seen again. Pale and shaking, Katie rocked back and forth, trying to get the image out of her head.

"Mom, are you coming?" Ashley asked.

Hearing a knock on her bedroom door, Katie was grateful for the distraction as Ashley became impatient.

"Mom, are you all right?" she asked.

"I'll be okay, honey. Can you get me some water, please?" Katie asked, ashamed of how she must have looked.

"Mom, please tell me what's wrong so I can help you!" Ashley said.

Katie explained to her what she had been going through the past year.

"Does anyone else know about this?" Ashley asked.

"Only your aunts and grandma. That's only because they have seen me pale," Katie said.

"Mom, I'm so sorry for you!" Ashley said, helping her mom up to get some water.

"Let me take a shower, and I will meet you downstairs, okay?" Katie said, slowly walking to get clean clothes.

"Okay, Mom. I'll see you in a little bit; I'm going to put a movie in and make some popcorn," Ashley said, walking out of her room.

After a long shower, Katie looked forward to having company downstairs. "Hey, Mom. I'm staying tonight, okay?" Ashley said, already comfortable on her couch.

"Okay, thanks!" Katie said, sitting down to take a break. Hanging out with her daughter helped her a lot.

Falling asleep on the couch, Katie woke up early for her morning jog. Coming back after a four-mile jog, "Good morning! It's Friday!" Katie said, feeling a lot better. Coming back in, sweaty from her jog, Katie woke up Ashley to have her eat breakfast before her models arrived.

"I know, and it's my day off, Mom," Ashley said, crawling off her couch.

Ashley fell asleep on the couch, watching a movie with her Mom.

"Hey, ladies. Good morning," Rachel and Casey said, walking in the front door.

Giving Ashley a hug, Rachel and Casey decided to come to work early in hopes of leaving early since it was their last day before vacation.

"A family breakfast!" Casey said, wishing Jacob and Devon were there for Katie too.

"Yes, let's enjoy this!" Rachel said, seeing how happy Katie looked after a hard week.

"Mom, I can help you today in the studio, if you would like; I don't have any big plans," Ashley said.

"Thanks, Ashley. I would love that!" her mom said.

"You know I love the camera as much as you do!" Ashley said, winking at her mom.

"Like I could forget," Katie said, heading downstairs to her studio, knowing Mark would be earlier than usual.

"Mom, I'll be back in an hour," Ashley said, cleaning up her mess and heading out the front door.

"Bye, Aunt Rachel and Aunt Casey. I'll say 'bye' before I leave for the day. I love you!" she said, closing the door behind her. With Katie running up to her room to grab her paperwork for her day, she stopped to look out her bay window across from her library.

"Katie, are you all right?" Rachel asked, seeing her looking very sad.

"Yes, just thinking, as usual. We are all truly blessed; God is so good to me!" Katie said, hugging her sister.

"I couldn't agree more!" Rachel said, heading back to her office.

Stopping by the library on her way back downstairs, Katie stopped to see her sisters hard at work. Always wrapped up in her studio, Katie forgot how much it took to run the book business. With only doing the finances, Katie hired her two younger sisters, Rachel and Casey, to work in the library upstairs and her Mom, Jackie to run the book factory one hour north from where Katie resided. Smiling, Katie went down her spiral stairs to pay Sheri, her chef for her hard work for that week, plus her vacation check for the following week.

"Good morning, boss!" she said, knowing when Mark called her that she would get a smile on her face.

"Here's your paycheck; thanks for everything!" Katie said, knowing she gave her a little bonus. Looking at her check, all Sheri could do was give her a hug. Knowing she struggled like Katie did as a single mother, Katie knew it would be appreciated.

"Thanks for being such a great boss," Sheri said, knowing God had blessed her as well. "You look like a new woman. Did you meet a nice man and forget to tell me?"

"No, Ashley spent the night, and she is spending her day off with me in the studio," Katie said.

Beep! Beep! she heard coming from her purse.

"Hey, boss. We just landed here; see you in twenty minutes," he said.

"Thanks, Mark!" Katie said, hurrying downstairs to get ready for her models.

Hearing them all come in the backdoor, Katie was excited her vacation would start at the end of the day.

Walking them downstairs, Mark wanted to see Katie. Always running around, he too was grateful for her as well.

"I'm here!" Ashley said.

"Hey, everyone! This is my daughter, Ashley, and she's a model as well," Katie said proudly. With Ashley blessed with all the same talents as her mother, their day flew by.

"Lunchtime!" they all heard from upstairs.

"Thanks, Sheri. We will be right up!" Katie said.

"Hey, Ashley, how have you been?" Mark said, giving her a hug. "You don't live far from here at all!"

"I've been doing really well, working a lot of hours in the jail and modeling on my weekends off," Ashley said, knowing her Mom did the same thing around her age.

Grabbing her cell phone, Katie had everyone go upstairs for lunch. Sitting at the huge kitchen table, Katie walked away to check her messages while she was working. Shocked to see another unknown number, Katie stepped outside for some privacy. Listening to her only voice mail, she was surprised to hear her modeling agent from fifteen years ago.

"Katie, it's Kelsey. I'm calling you about a modeling job. Please call me back; I've missed you!" she said. Knowing she had a few minutes to call her back, Katie was curious about her assignment. Calling her back, Katie was thrilled to hear her upbeat sense of humor.

"Miss Katie, how have you been?" she said.

"I've been great, and yourself?" Katie said excitedly.

"Well, this is short notice, but I entered your pictures in a contest for women that have been in the modeling industry over twenty years, and they picked you and nine other women," Kelsey said. "I have to get off here; my plane is getting ready to leave. I'll call you this evening with the details."

Overwhelmed with emotion, Katie tried to contain herself as she walked back into the kitchen.

"Mom, who was that? You have a huge smile on your face," Ashley said, knowing her models were there. Being a private and professional woman, Ashley knew that it wasn't the time to discuss her personal life. "Can we talk in private please?"

Ashley wondered why her Mom had such a huge smile on her face from just a phone call. Talking for just a few minutes, Katie told her daughter briefly about her phone call from Kelsey. Coming back into the kitchen, Katie ate lunch with her models and Ashley, then headed back down to her studio to finish up her day.

"I'll go see if Rachel and Casey are hungry; they rarely come down for lunch," Sheri said, trying to change the subject.

"Okay, we have to get back down to the studio to finish our day," Katie said, cleaning off her plate. With the models following her lead, they all went back to work, knowing there were only a few models left to do their photo shoots.

CHAPTER 2

With Ashley's help, the rest of her workday seemed to fly by. Katie wondered why she didn't hire her to work in the studio. Anxious to call Kelsey back, Katie walked her models upstairs to meet Mark. Walking back downstairs, Katie watched Ashley cleaning up from the long day. Knowing she wanted to move to California with Devon, Katie didn't want to make her feel obligated to stay in Missouri to run the photography business.

"Hey, Ashley. I have an idea," her mom said, expecting her to say no. "Do you want to work as my assistant? I think it would help with my stress level."

"Mom, I think that's a great idea, but let me think about it while you're on vacation, okay?" Ashley said, thrilled she offered her the opportunity.

"Fair enough," Katie said, getting out her cell phone to call Kelsey back. "Hey, Kelsey. Thanks for the call earlier; I'm excited!" Katie said, shocked Kelsey thought of her.

"Hey, Miss Katie. The photo shoot is tomorrow in Jacksonville, Florida, does that pose a problem?" she asked.

"No, that doesn't pose a problem at all," Katie said. "Where do you need me to be, and what time?"

"Same resort we did your photo shoot many years ago, and if you could, please be there by ten in the morning; we meet the photographer at five o'clock," Kelsey said, thrilled the magazine picked Katie out of thousands of other models.

"Sounds good; see you there!" Katie said as she went to help Ashley clean up her studio.

"So, tell me about what Kelsey said," Ashley said curiously. Telling her the great news, Katie thanked her for all her hard work.

"Sure thing, Mom. I had a lot of fun!" Ashley said, getting ready to head to her house.

"Well, Kelsey, my modeling agent from several years ago, called and wants me to fly to Florida for a photo shoot; she submitted my pictures and resume for models that have been successful for over twenty years!" Katie said, sounding like a young child in a candy store.

"Mom, that's an honor. Congratulations! If anyone deserves something like this, it's you for sure!" Ashley said, hugging her Mother.

"I love you, and I'll call you next week. Maybe you can have Mark fly you down to the beach house for a couple days while I'm on vacation," Katie said, trying not to push her luck.

"I would enjoy that," Ashley said, smiling. Walking her outside, Katie couldn't believe her eyes at how much she had matured as a woman.

Heading to her office on the main floor to make sure everything was taken care of while she was away in Florida, Katie grabbed her phone from her side to call Mark to make arrangements to fly the next morning to Jacksonville to meet Kelsey, and then she would have Brandon pick her up from the airport a day early. With her beach house in the same city, Katie felt a sense of relief.

Sitting at her desk, Katie suddenly realized she was all alone again. Staring around her office, Katie decided to call Brandon at the beach house to give him plenty of notice.

"Hey, stranger!" Katie said, hearing his friendly voice.

"Hey, Katie! How have you been?" he said.

"I've been busy, as usual. The reason I'm calling is I need you to pick me up in the limousine tomorrow at the airport, then take me to Royal Resort; I have a photo shoot with my modeling agent from many years ago," Katie said, already excited.

"Sounds good. I'll see you then. I'll call you on my way," Brandon said.

"Okay, thanks. I'll talk to you later," Katie said, getting up to pack for both of her trips.

Tired from a long week, Katie headed upstairs to take a shower and get ready for an exciting day at the resort. Turning the music on to keep her mind from wandering, Katie packed two separate bags: one for the resort, and the other for vacation. A low-maintained woman, even with millions of dollars, Katie still longed for the simple things in life. Looking around her walk-in closet, Katie was amazed at all the clothes, shoes, and purses, all organized by color. Always a bargain shopper, Katie took pride in all the things she was able to collect over the years.

Bored, she decided to write in her journal. Keeping her thoughts written down helped her get her feelings out. Overwhelmed most of the time, Katie was grateful for her many talents. Hearing the phone ring, Katie was surprised to see it was her Mother calling.

"Hey, sweetie. I'm on my way over," Jackie said, knowing it had been a week since she had seen Katie.

"Great! I'll make something to eat," Katie told her, heading downstairs.

Excited about all the good news, Katie went in her living room to watch some news. Knowing the outside world was always chaotic, Katie tried to help others that were less fortunate. Giving her money to several charities, Katie wanted to watch better things happen for the new generation.

Making salads for each of them, she heard a knock on the front door.

"Come in!" Katie yelled, knowing it was Jackie.

"Hey, sweetie," she said, meeting her in the kitchen. "Are you ready for vacation?" Jackie said, knowing she was just as excited.

"Yes, I have a photo shoot in Florida tomorrow with Kelsey, so I'm going to stay until Sunday and have

Brandon pick me up," Katie said, trying to keep her excitement under control.

"Good for you!" her mom said, sitting down to eat her salad with her daughter. "Sam is coming back tomorrow from Iowa, then we are off to the Bahamas on Monday for a week," Jackie said excitedly. "I think we are all ready for a much needed break!" she said, knowing Katie had to be overwhelmed after working so many hours every day.

Catching up on everything from the week, Katie decided to get some sleep to get up early for her flight. Grateful, Katie was so happy to have such a healthy relationship with all of her family.

Heading up to her room to get ready for bed, Katie shut the bathroom door and stopped in her tracks. Sitting down on her floor, Katie felt as if she were drunk. Rocking back and forth, she tried to contain herself, scared of having an anxiety attack. Katie saw an image of a woman who was in her late forties with big glasses and a huge head of curly hair. Standing only four feet nine inches, Katie couldn't imagine the crime she would commit. A happily married couple would hire a nurse to stay at home with her disabled husband while she was working to pay the bills. Little did she know the nurse would shoot her point-blank, killing her instantly, in broad daylight.

"Katie, are you okay in there?" Jackie asked, hearing things fall from upstairs.

"Go away, please!" Katie said, knowing she looked affright.

"No, I want to help you!" her mom said, trying to get the door unlocked.

"I'll be right out, Mom," Katie said, splashing water on her face.

"Oh my gosh, Katie. You look like you saw a ghost," Jackie said, knowing she had episodes sometimes. "Can I get you anything?"

With a shake of her head, Jackie knew that was her cue to get her some cold water and a cool washcloth.

"I'm not doing anything tonight. If you want me to stay in the extra room, I will," Jackie said, hoping she would take her up on her offer. "I will even stay up and put in a good movie to take your mind off everything. Deal?"

"Mom, I would like that, thanks, but I can't stay up too late because I'm flying out at eight in the morning," Katie said, knowing she would have images all night of that woman's face. "I'm going to throw myself together real fast; I'll be done in about thirty minutes, okay? Thanks! I love you!"

"Okay, I'm going to my house and doing the same thing. I'll be back by the time you get done," Jackie said.

"I'll be fine, Mom. Sorry to frighten you," Katie said, closing her bathroom door gently.

After a long shower, Katie felt like a new woman. Heading downstairs to start a movie, Katie heard her mom come in the backdoor.

"Hey, honey! I'm back!" She was always happy, no matter the situation. "Are you excited about your first photo shoot in years?" Jackie asked, excited for her, knowing it was a passion of hers since she was a young child. Going to auditions since age fifteen, Katie was encouraged to follow her dreams.

"Yes, I'm shocked, but thrilled!" Katie said, calming herself down more.

"Good. Do you think these episodes are caused from stress?" her mom asked.

"I'm not sure what makes it happen, but I see the scariest things," Katie said, wanting to change the subject. "Everything seems fine one minute, and like a flash of lightning, I see scary people's faces and the horrible things they have done in that part of their lives. I don't know how to describe it, but it's very traumatic to me. I mean, it almost feels like I'm standing there at that time watching these horrible acts happen right before my eyes."

Enjoying the rest of their night, Katie fell asleep on the couch, knowing the next day would be stressful.

The next morning, Katie woke up at the crack of dawn and got ready for her morning jog. Enjoying her four-mile run, Katie felt as if she needed a structured routine to keep self-confidence alive.

Coming back in, Katie went upstairs to take a shower and get ready for her adventure with Kelsey. *Beep! Beep!*

"Good morning, sunshine!" Mark said, knowing he had to leave in a couple of hours to take her to Florida.

"Good morning. Thanks for the call, but I have been up since dawn," Katie said, amazed at her own confidence.

"Hey, can I ask you a question?" Mark said, nervous. "I need to ask you a question and I know it may seem like an odd request, but can I use your jet to fly my family to London please, it will be a great feeling to fly straight through!"

To his amazement, Katie didn't hesitate as he was a very trustworthy man.

"Sure, anything," Katie said.

"Yes, that's fine. Please pick me up at the airport next Sunday, though," Katie said.

"Thanks. We will be spoiled flying straight through," Mark said, shocked she didn't even hesitate. Trusting him, Katie had no reservations letting his family and him take their first trip to London.

"Mom!" Katie said, shaking her.

"Yes, sweetie?" Jackie said.

Moving around trying to wake herself up, Jackie opened her eyes, grateful to see Katie back to her normal self.

"I'm leaving in an hour or so for Florida. You want to eat breakfast together before I leave?" Katie said, knowing she would miss her.

"Sure, I'll meet you in the kitchen, okay?" Jackie said, worried about Katie being alone all week in her huge beach house.

Carrying her bags downstairs for her trip, Katie made a quick meal to spend a little more time with her mother, who she rarely got to spend any mother-daughter time with.

"Mom, thanks for staying here last night," Katie said, letting her emotions get the best of her. "It was great to have your company as always; I never figured I would miss my kids this much!"

"I enjoyed it as much as you did," Jackie said, knowing Sam was still away, visiting his family up north. "You know I worry about you a lot." her mom said as she kissed her on the forehead.

"I know, but you don't have to, really; I'll be fine," Katie said, hearing Mark pull up outside.

"Have a great time on your vacation, Katie," Jackie said. "It's well deserved!"

"Thanks. I'm going to hang out with Brandon. I'm sure he gets really bored in that beach house alone," Katie said, already excited yet still nervous about her photo shoot before her vacation would even start.

"I'm sure Brandon will be happy to see you. He's like one of our own family members," Jackie said, remembering Brandon when he and her grandson, Jacob, would be in middle school together.

Grabbing her bags, Katie headed outside to meet Mark with her luggage.

"Hey, Jackie. How have you been?" Mark said, surprised to see her.

"Good. I came to hang out with Katie before she left," she said, hugging her daughter good-bye.

"Thanks, Mom. I love you. Have fun in the Bahamas with Sam," Katie said, knowing she had to stay on schedule.

Riding in the truck to the jet, Katie didn't remember all the land that was all hers. Her little jogs every day were so routine for her she never took the time out to ride her four-wheeler on her property. Not seeing her jet in so long, Katie's eyes had to adjust to the reality that is was hers. It was huge jet with a television and video games to make the time go by faster.

Katie watched Mark load her bags. "Wow, I need to get out more," Katie said to Mark. Not seeing her private jet since she bought it a year prior, Katie's eyes had to adjust to the idea that it was hers.

"I don't remember this being so big!" Katie said, finding a place to sit with a lot of seats and a large screen television for long flights.

"Yes, you do. You spend way too much time in your house," Mark said, feeling bad for her, knowing she had to be lost without her kids. "Ready? It's a short flight. No worries; you're in good hands," he said, flashing his big smile.

"Thanks. I trust you," she said to Mark as the door closed.

Frozen, Katie saw a young man, only in his late teens coming home from school, shocked to see his mother and sister shot to death by his father, still holding the rifle. Scared, the young man would run to the neighbors for help. Sparing the young man's life, he would show up with the police to find his father dead as well from a self-inflicted shot to his head.

"Katie, are you ignoring me?" Mark asked, trying to catch her attention.

"No, I'm sorry, Mark. I was just thinking," Katie said, still shocked at the crazy things her eyes would have to witness. "How long until we land?"

"We only have a half hour left," Mark said, unsure of her silence most of the flight.

Always a talkative person, Katie caught herself going to places in her mind that only people would see in their nightmares.

"Okay, thanks!" Katie said, grabbing her newest book she started writing. "Thanks for a being such a great friend to me and my family; it would never be the same without you."

"The feeling is mutual, really. Thanks again from myself and my family!" Mark said, preparing for landing. "Brandon should be here soon to take you to the resort," he said.

"Thanks. You pick up a lot of my slack," Katie said, smiling.

"No, we just work well together," he said, getting quiet while he landed the jet. Mark had been laid off from an automotive plant. He flew as a hobby until he met Katie through a mutual friend. With the economy in recession back then, Mark needed to find some stability for his family. His wife, Jennifer, worked as a nurse for a local hospital to keep their heads above water. Katie offering him the job as her pilot made all the difference to them.

"Miss Katie, we are here!" Mark said.

"Thanks, Mark. You were right; the flight went by fast," she said, smiling.

"That's because you were daydreaming most of the trip," Mark said.

"I'm sorry, Mark," Katie said, knowing her secret would stay between just them. "My mind tends to wonder from time to time. It's something beyond my control that I'm hoping will go away sometime in the near future."

Grabbing all of her belongings, Katie tried to stay focused on her work with Kelsey. Getting up, Katie saw the door open as Mark stood there smiling.

"Good luck today!" Mark said, helping her grab her things.

"Thanks, it's been a while since I was in front of the camera," she said.

"You're beautiful, Katie. Don't forget that." Mark said, trying to boost her self-esteem.

"Thanks. Some days I just feel blah," Katie said, grabbing her purse.

"It will get better; today is a new day, and you're in sunny Florida!" he said, trying to make her smile.

Turning her cell phone on, Katie looked for Brandon's number. "Hey, Brandon. Where are you?" Katie said.

"Pulling into the airport, boss," Brandon said. Grabbing her bags, Mark walked over to her and gave her a hug. Standing six feet three inches, Katie felt like a little kid again.

Pulling up to Katie and Mark, Brandon got out to load up her belongings.

"Good to see you again!" Brandon said, always grateful for everything she did for him.

"Katie, I'm going to head back home," Mark said, waving goodbye. "Have a great photo shoot, and enjoy your vacation. I'll see you here next Sunday."

Loading up in her limousine, Katie was excited about her next adventure. "So Katie, to the resort, right?" Brandon asked. He always looked up to her for all her determination, from raising her kids alone to successfully running two businesses out of her house. Brandon, a friend of Jacob's growing up, lost his wife and two kids in a fatal car crash by a drunk driver while he was at work one stormy evening. Around the same time, Katie was designing her dream house. Watching Brandon struggle day by day, she decided to put him to work by hiring him to make sure her house was built properly. With her businesses booming, Katie decided to buy the beach house in Florida as a getaway place for her and her family. A five-bedroom house on the ocean made a great place to breathe. With Brandon alone a lot, Katie offered him to live there rent-free. With driving her limousine on the side, Brandon worked as a carpenter. Making enough to pay the utilities and maintenance, Brandon was given a sense of independence. Always grateful for her generosity, Brandon knew she was an angel from above looking down on him and smiling. As Brandon closed the limousine door, Katie felt like a diva, something she rarely ever felt like.

"So, Katie, we are off to the resort correct?" he asked, always happy to see her. What always seemed like a second mom to him, Brandon envied the things Katie would go through to keep her family as normal and drama-free as possible.

"Yes, I'm going to meet my modeling agent for a photo shoot. I need you to pick me up at the resort when I'm ready to head to the beach house, please!" Katie said, still very excited about the chance to get her own portfolio updated after several years.

"Well, Katie, we are almost there," Brandon said with a smile. "It's great to see you as always!"

Brandon, a friend of Jacob's since middle school would grow up to marry his college sweetheart and have two precious children. A proud man, Brandon would go to work as a carpenter for a huge company out of St. Louis; after several years, he went to work one stormy day only to find out his family was killed in a fatal car accident by a drunk driver. Never the same after that, Katie would see his potential and watch Brandon's life crumble around him. Designing her own house as a teenager, Katie would fulfill her dreams as her businesses financially took off like a summer breeze. Putting Brandon in charge of all of the work, she asked Brandon to hire the crews he knew that would make sure the job was done right.

"So any big plans for your week?" Brandon asked, trying to make casual conversation.

"Hopefully the girls will fly down for a couple of days. Jacob is still on tour, and he has a girlfriend," Katie said, still shocked a girl answered his phone.

"Good for him. He deserves to be happy after all he has been through," Brandon said.

"Yes, things have been good for all of us lately," Katie said as they pulled up to the resort.

"Here you are!" Brandon said.

As Brandon got out to open the door for her, Katie felt like a diva. Rarely getting out, Katie had a huge smile on her face while she put on her sunglasses.

"Well, Katie, have fun. You deserve to be pampered. You're always taking care of everyone else; this week is all about you!" he said, grabbing her bag for the overnight stay. "Call me when you're ready to be picked up tomorrow, okay?" he said, smiling.

A nice-looking young man, Katie knew someday he would able to move on with his life. With only being a couple of years since the loss of his family, Katie hoped someday he would find some sense of happiness within himself.

"Okay. Thanks, Brandon. I'll call you tomorrow, and thanks again; you're the best!" Katie said, heading in the door to see if Kelsey had reserved her a room.

Amazed at all the changes, Katie felt a sense of relief already. "Ms. Roth, here's your key, and the bellboy will walk your bags up with you to your room. Have a great stay," the woman said. She was so nice and friendly.

"Thanks so much, and have a blessed day!" Katie said, smiling, as she followed the young man to the elevators. Hearing her phone go off, Katie reached inside her Chanel purse to see if Kelsey had arrived yet.

"Hello, Katie. Have you made it to the resort yet?" Kelsey asked.

"Yes, I'm on the way to my room now as we speak," Katie said, very excited to be back to a place that was full of good times, yet she was still in a hectic time of her life.

"I'll meet you in the lobby at one o'clock for lunch and plenty of details, okay?" Kelsey said, boarding her plane. "I'm leaving St. Louis now. See you soon!" Kelsey said.

Little did she know the young, aspiring model would work for her for six years. Both single mothers, they formed a bond that would last forever.

"Ma'am, enjoy your stay," the bellboy said, trying to catch her attention.

"Thanks for everything!" Katie said as she gave him a fifty dollar tip.

"Thanks, and have a great stay!" the young man said, shocked to get such a big tip. As he walked out of her room, Katie heard the door slam.

"No, not today!" Katie said as she sat on her bed.

Phone ring or something, she thought. *Please, anything.*

Scared she would have another episode, Katie tried to keep herself contained.

Walking outside to the balcony, she felt a sense of hope. *I did it!* Katie thought, relieved she was able to focus on the sound of the ocean waves. Knowing she had a couple of hours before Kelsey arrived, Katie put on her comfortable clothes for a nice walk on the beach.

Seeing happy couples, Katie wondered why God had blessed her with everything else but a good man that would accept her for who she was. Looking at the time, she realized it was almost time to meet Kelsey. Heading back to her room to get ready for lunch, Katie forgot the door slams when it closes. Stopping in place, she felt herself spinning as if she were drunk. Shaky and pale, Katie walked over to her bed, trying to gather herself before she got worse. Seeing a man in his forties standing six feet seven inches and very slim, Katie would see his face and shake even more. A man that would date a woman his age for many years would suddenly decide one day to do the unthinkable. Taking a sixteen-year-old girl for what she thought would be an errand would turn out to be a nightmare only several minutes later. Having a bag full of fantasies, the man would rape her several times before realizing what he was doing was wrong. Sparing her life, he would drive her home as if he did nothing wrong. Arrested days later, the man, still without guilt, would hopefully spend the rest of his life behind bars, sparing other teenagers the fear that he would be walking the streets, looking for his next victim.

Knock! Knock!

"Katie, it's Kelsey!" she heard as she rushed to the mirror to see how she looked.

She can't see me like this! she thought as she splashed water on her face and brushed her hair quickly. Answering the door, Katie tried to pretend that what she saw would not show up on her face.

"Katie, it's one-thirty. What happened?" Kelsey said, worried about her friend.

"Sorry, I got distracted. It will only take me a few minutes to get ready for lunch," Katie said, rushing around the room.

"It's all right; I'm in no hurry. It's the photographer we have to be on time for," Kelsey said, giving Katie a hug.

"Thanks for understanding. I'm so excited!" Katie said, starting to feel like herself again.

"No problem. I'm just glad you were able to make it on such short notice," Kelsey said, knowing Katie was always spontaneous.

Throwing some nice clothes and makeup on real quickly, Katie decided a ponytail would have to do. "I'm ready when you are," Katie said, bouncing back to her normal self again.

"Let's go, my diva!" Kelsey said.

"I'm not a diva, really," Katie said, being modest.

"Yes, you are, but with a lot of class," Kelsey said, knowing how successful she was. "I know what you have been doing, Miss Katie," she said.

"You do?" Katie said, shocked.

"I am a modeling agent, and good news travels fast, my dear. I couldn't be more proud of you!" Kelsey said as they headed to a restaurant for lunch.

Eating, Katie and Kelsey caught up on each other's lives. Although both were very busy, they still tried to keep some sort of contact.

"I saw your Web site, and I sometimes send models to apply. I love your work and how you maintain your business. Very classy," Kelsey said.

"Thanks," Katie said. "So about the shoot today, what it is for?"

"I submitted some of your work to a contest for models that have been in the business for twenty years or longer," Kelsey said. "I thought of you instantly, and once they responded, I contacted you!"

Kelsey remembered Katie very young and trying to get into the modeling industry with very little money. Kelsey, not an agent very long at that time either, met Katie and had seen potential in her that she couldn't see in herself.

"There are ten models trying out for two spots to Italy for a cover and the models background from the beginning until now!" Kelsey said.

"Thanks, Kelsey, for believing in me even after all these years. It's a blessing all by itself," Katie said, smiling back at her.

"I brought some wardrobe for you to pick from, lady. I hope you like them. This trip is casual wear, unlike before—you were wearing a swimsuit," Kelsey said, remembering the day like it was yesterday.

"Thanks for everything. I'm nervous yet excited all at the same time," Katie said, knowing she could be herself around Kelsey.

"You will do fine; this is what you're meant to do, in front of and behind the camera. Don't ever doubt yourself; I have seen you overcome what most women wished they were strong enough to do," Kelsey said, always giving her encouragement. "I'll see you at my room at four o'clock, and don't be a minute late, please!" Kelsey said, knowing she was ready for a nap after such a long week.

Walking into her room, Katie shut the door as quietly as she could without triggering another episode. Always an outgoing woman, Katie always had a shy side as well, not sure if it came from her past from all the abuse she suffered as a child until adulthood. Trying to hide her pain with a smile became something Katie knew all too well, from seeing her friends from school go in and out of prison for unthinkable crimes. Katie couldn't figure out how she was so blessed to not have the same mentality, even with all the trauma suffered growing up—learning at a young age to battle things most adults couldn't. Seeing people close to her die at a young age to grown adults getting into a fatal accident just trying to make it home to their loved ones. Walking around her room, Katie started to feel anxious. She decided to call her kids; she always knew they could give her just enough moral support with just a few words. A mother raising her kids alone most of their lives, Katie tried to give them as normal life as possible. With peer pressures of their own, Katie hoped and prayed they would follow their hearts and stick to their dreams. What seemed easy to Katie when her kids were small would hit a huge road block with her teenagers dealing with life from different views with many medical problems from mental to chemical dependency, something many other people related to. Always praying her kids would overcome their own demons, Katie watched them jump hurdles throughout school, learning no matter what the situation was, always try to make it right when they made a bad choice and not dwell on the past. A lesson even Katie herself had trouble doing from time to time.

Going through her phone, she realized she had a missed call. Listening to her voice mail, she heard Caleb's voice again.

"I know I'm the last person you want to hear from, but I just wanted to apologize for all the hurt I caused you many years ago. Please, call me back."

Shocked, Katie called him back for her own closure. Ringing a few times, Katie almost hung up.

"Hi, Caleb," Katie said, still unsure what to say. "How have you been doing? It's been many years since I've heard your voice."

"I've been doing pretty good," Caleb said. "I'm still in the army. I decided to retire from here. I think I was meant to be a fighter."

"So, I don't mean to be so blunt, but why are you calling me after all these years?" Katie asked him, wanting to know the truth.

"I know I did a lot of things in my past I'm not proud of and losing you the way I did was one of them," Caleb said, truly sincere. "I just called to tell you I'm sorry. I hope some day you will forgive me for treating you the way I did, by making you believe I was only dating you at the time."

Katie felt uncomfortable from all the old feelings coming back.

"Caleb, thanks for the phone call and you admitting what you did was wrong," Katie said "I forgive you." Katie knew she would never have trust in him again, but at the same time, she was grateful he finally felt bad after all the years that had past.

"I've been good. I got remarried and gained full custody of my daughter," he said, trying to keep the conversation going.

"Congrats to you, and thanks for calling. I really need to get off here though," Katie said, trying not to sound rude.

"Okay, Katie. Take care!" he said, wanting closure himself, knowing he broke her heart many years ago without an explanation.

Confused, Katie called Devon first. Sitting in her bed, Katie grabbed her photo album out of her purse, wanting to look at pictures of her kids. Smiling, she heard Devon's voice.

"Hey, Mom. How are you?" she said, always happy to talk to her mother.

"Good. I have a photo shoot here in Florida with Kelsey soon, and I just wanted to have your moral support. It's still needed time to time, even though you are grown now," Katie said, laughing, wishing she were really there to wish her good luck.

"Mom, you have my support, but you are a natural in front of the camera and behind. 'No worries' is what you always tell me!" Devon said.

"Thanks. You always make me smile and always have faith in me. I hope to see you at the beach house a couple days next week," Katie said.

"I'll see what I can do, okay?" Devon said, saying her good-byes for now.

Dialing Ashley, Katie hoped she would work for her in her studio.

"Hey, Ashley. It's almost time for my photo shoot. I just wanted to hear your voice!" Katie said, amazed at the mature adult Ashley turned out to be.

"Have fun! You will do great, as always!" Ashley said, trying to make her feel better.

"Thanks. I hope you can make it down here while I'm at the beach house," Katie said, trying not to make her feel guilty.

"I will see what's going on here at home, okay? I love you. Bye, for now," Ashley said.

A little nervous about calling Jacob, Katie called him, knowing he could boost her self-esteem by a simple "I love you."

"Hello, Mom. Is everything okay?" he asked, worried she called twice in the same week.

"Yes, I'm great. I'm getting ready for my photo shoot, and I haven't had one of them for many years," Katie said, trying not to sound pathetic.

"Mom, you are one of the strongest women I have ever met. You were meant to shine," he said, so grateful for all of the things she did for him growing up.

A single mother since Jacob was fourteen, Katie would go without many things to give her kids a simple life. "Hearing all three of you kids is what I think I needed," Katie said.

"Hey, aren't you in Florida at the beach house for a week's vacation?" Jacob asked.

"Yes, I'm not sure what I'm going to do, but relaxing sounds nice," Katie said, trying to make him smile.

"You're right. You need to treat yourself and take Brandon out to dinner. I'm sure he will enjoy your company," Jacob said, being more talkative than usual.

"Thanks. I will let you go; I need to call Kelsey to find out what's going on," Katie said, telling him her good-byes.

"Love you, Mom. Have fun!" he said, ending the conversation.

Four o'clock already. Great, I managed to keep myself awake, and now ready for some great pictures for the photographer.

CHAPTER 3

Calling Kelsey, she decided she was ready to see what she would be wearing.

"Come on over to my room. I will show you," Kelsey said.

"Okay, let me freshen up my makeup and hair. I'll be over there soon," Katie said, heading to her big makeup case. With her high cheekbones and thin lips, Katie strived harder to keep her complexion looking young. With hair halfway down her back, Katie liked her straight hair over her shoulders. Heading out with her makeup case and purse, Katie was confident she could do it like she did before.

Knock! Knock!

"Hey, you look great! Here are your clothes to pick from. The bathroom is right around the corner."

Shutting the door behind her, Katie felt her head spinning. Seeing a fragile lady's face, detoxing from alcohol, Katie felt her legs go limp. Sitting on the floor, Katie started to panic.

"Katie, are you all right?" Kelsey asked, hearing her talk to herself.

"Yes, I'll be right out," Katie said, trying to get that woman's face out of her head. Still shaky, Katie was grateful for the distraction.

Walking out still sweaty, Kelsey worried about her again. "Are you sure you're up for this?" Kelsey asked.

I have this problem that is very odd," Katie said. "I'm really embarrassed to share this with you, but I feel the need to inform you as my agent and my friend that sometimes when doors shut behind me, I see the craziest things. Sometimes I can't even explain them!"

"I understand, and thank you for being honest with me. We can work through this," Kelsey said, helping her fix her hair and makeup again after shaking and sweating.

"Thanks. I knew you would relate to my problem," Katie said, trying not to tear up.

"I do, and it will get better," Kelsey said, liking the dark jeans and the solid pink shirt she had picked from the pile. Usually wearing black or brown, Katie learned to put some color to make her personality come out more. "You can grab some flip flops if you want, but at your shoot, you will be barefoot to make the scene more natural."

Grabbing her things, Katie followed Kelsey down to the lobby to meet her photographer.

"You look great!" Kelsey said, amazed at the things Katie had to deal with. "It's no wonder with what your eyes have seen that you are still able to be successful." Kelsey gave Katie a much-needed hug.

"Let's do this!" Katie said, feeling as if she was in her twenties again. Standing in the sand, posing, Katie had no problems relaxing for the camera. An hour seemed to fly by as she changed her clothes and hair a few times. Going out to the beach close to the ocean, Katie stood in many positions to get several angels of her face, hair and body, knowing all the pictures would be needed to find a few good ones to be submitted. With her long brown hair blowing in the wind, Katie started to get more comfortable in front of the camera again.

"You're doing a great job, Katie," Shawn, the photographer said. " I see you're a natural at this. I'm very impressed!"

Seeing her shy side in the beginning was fading fast as she fell right back into routine.

"That's a wrap! Great job!" the photographer said.

Looking at the pictures, Katie was shocked at the wrinkles under her eyes.

"You look great, Katie!" Kelsey said.

"Thanks. Do you really think they turned out well?" Katie asked, needing some reassurance.

"You did well. I liked it a lot; I knew I would," Kelsey said to her, amazed at her professionalism. "I'm going to send some of these off tonight. No worries; they are awesome!"

"They are pretty good, huh?" Katie said, trying not to sound conceited.

REBEKAH ROSS

"There you go. It's just been too long since you were in front of the camera," Kelsey told her, knowing she used to update her pictures twice a year. "Time to celebrate!"

She took Katie out to dinner. Catching up on more of their lives, Katie took out her laptop to show Kelsey both of her businesses.

"I'm very impressed at all your hard work. You have to be one of the most dedicated people I know," Kelsey said, somewhat envious of her.

"Thanks. God has blessed me with a strong will," Katie said, toasting a glass of wine. Never a big drinker, Katie had watched alcohol ruin many people's lives.

"I need to hop a plane back to St. Louis. Good luck to you, and we will be in touch within the next week or so," Kelsey said as they headed back to their rooms.

"Thanks for everything, really; it's been a lot of fun!" Katie said, having had such a good photo shoot. Katie decided since she was exhausted and it was getting late that it would be best just to enjoy the resort one last night. Walking into her room, Katie felt confident for once. Getting all her clothes ready for her shower, Katie closed the door behind her. Spinning, Katie saw a woman with long, bleach-blonde hair wandering the streets, high on drugs, not aware of her surroundings. She would walk into a gas station and try to use cigarettes for money to pay for gas that she didn't even have. Alerting authorities, the woman would be rushed to a mental hospital by an ambulance. Wondering how someone could have behavior like that, Katie just shook her head, ashamed for the people such as herself that would struggle through life sober.

Gathering herself, Katie tried to catch her breath. Trying to relax, she was beginning to get worried about her own mental health. Wondering if she had post-traumatic stress syndrome, Katie hoped for a good week at her beach house. Sitting out on her balcony in her robe, Katie decided to try to get some sleep. Crawling into her big bed, Katie flipped through the channels on her big television. Grabbing her cell phone, Katie saw she missed a few calls from her family. Late, Katie decided to call them back and tell them the good news about her photo shoot. Talking on the phone to her sisters, she already felt back at home.

"Have fun at the beach house, sis. You will enjoy the change of scenery," Rachel said, telling her good-bye.

Laying her head down on her fluffy pillow, Katie fell fast asleep. Always a sleepwalker, she caught herself wandering around her suite. Wishing she could have a normal life she had dreamed of since a child, Katie stayed confident the images of strangers would go away and never come back. Rocking back and forth, she looked at the time on her clock. *Four o'clock in the morning*, she thought, knowing everyone would be asleep. Lonely, Katie wandered out to the balcony to listen to the waves down below.

Hearing people outside partying like it was ten o'clock at night, all she could do was wonder why she was spared that lifestyle. She knew she liked being a positive role model. Katie, trying to relax again, laid her head back down and closed her eyes. Opening them quickly, she saw a man's face staring back at her. Jumping out of her skin, she realized there was nobody but her in her hotel room. Knowing it was too early to call Brandon, Katie walked down to the lobby to talk to the front-desk person. Scared to be left alone after all of her visions of that man's face, Katie, half asleep, went to the elevators and headed downstairs to enjoy the sounds of the waves from the ocean.

"Ma'am, are you all right?" the woman behind the front desk asked, seeing she wasn't fully awake.

"Yes, I just wanted to enjoy my last night here, but thanks for asking," Katie said, confused at her response.

Feeling as if she looked crazy and half asleep, Katie walked outside to put her feet in the sand. Sitting down, Katie loved the peace and quiet since everyone had fallen asleep.

"Ma'am, are you all right?" a man asked, wondering why she was outside in her nightclothes.

"Yes, I just couldn't sleep, and this view is so nice." Watching the sun come up, Katie wished she had a man that could always make her smile, no matter what the case.

Wandering back to her room, Katie called Brandon, ready to go to the beach house.

"Hello?" she heard. She woke him up. "Is everything okay?" Brandon asked, shocked she called so early in the morning.

"Yes and no. Can you come and pick me up, please?" Katie asked, wondering if she was going to be all right.

"I'll be there in thirty minutes. Please meet me out front," Brandon said.

Gathering her belongings, Katie went to the lobby to return her key. Walking outside and down a long flight of stairs to the pick-up area, Katie sat on her bag, waiting for Brandon. Pulling up in his Mustang, Brandon jumped out of the car to check on her.

"Katie, are you sure you are all right? Do you want me to stay at he beach house with you for the week so you have some company?" he asked her.

"No, I will be all right. Maybe we can do dinner a few nights, though," Katie said, trying not to sound rude.

"Okay. That sounds fine to me," Brandon said, loading her bags and closing the door behind her. "Katie, I'm worried about you. I've never seen this side of you in all the years I've known your family."

"I will be okay, Brandon. It's a long story, but I'm very confident it will work its way out somehow," Katie said, confusing him even more.

"Okay," he said. "Do you want to go out for breakfast?" Brandon asked, trying to keep her from being stuck in the beach house alone.

"Sure. That's a great idea!" Katie said. "Wait. I have to go to the house and change; I look affright!"

"Sure thing, Miss Katie. I sure have missed you!" he said.

"Thanks, Brandon," she said. "I've missed you too, and by the way, sorry to scare you this morning. I have been dealing with some personal issues within myself, and I'm hoping and praying some day they will get better on their own."

Katie wasn't sure if he understood any of what she was trying to say.

"It's all right, Katie, as long as you're going to get through this," Brandon said. "I'm here as your friend if you ever need anything. Okay. Here we are."

Brandon pulled up to the beach house.

"It looks different," Katie said, not realizing all the work he had done to the house.

"Yes, I got bored and planted some flowers, among other things," he said, smiling.

"It looks great!" she said, smiling. "I'm impressed, Brandon; you are truly talented!"

"We all have special talent, Katie. Some people never truly know their own talent," Brandon said, knowing Katie was talented in many ways.

Unloading her bags, Brandon asked her if she wanted a tour.

"Sure. This is such a surprise," Katie said, amazed at all the woodwork he had done. Looking around, Katie saw pictures of Brandon's family in the living room. With her mind still in a depressive state, Katie looked at some of her own pictures. Remembering back to when times were really rough, Katie wished she could lead a normal, happy life.

"Brandon, thanks for putting life into this beautiful house; it needed a special touch," Katie said, amazed at all his hard work.

"Whenever you're ready to go eat, I'll meet you outside. I'm staying at the local hotel for the week," Brandon said, giving her space to relax.

"Okay. I'll be done in a few minutes," Katie said, trying to keep her emotions under control.

"Sounds good, and cheer up, Katie. You have such a great life!" he said, smiling.

"You're right, Brandon. I miss my outgoing personality," Katie said, knowing he was like a son to her.

Walking into her room, Katie looked around, feeling like a stranger in her own place. Only staying a couple times at her beach house, Katie forgot how nice it was. With Brandon alone all the time, it was no wonder he would use his creative side.

Getting ready really quickly, Katie got dressed in shorts and a nice shirt. Taking a deep breath, Katie did her makeup and hair.

I can do this! she thought to herself, feeling more confident.

Going downstairs to meet Brandon, Katie smiled and put on her sunglasses. "I'm finally ready; it's such a nice day out!" Katie said, enjoying the scenery.

"Yes, you're in Florida, my dear; good weather all year round," Brandon said, trying to make her feel better. "You are so blessed, Katie," he opened her limousine door for her.

"Let's take your car; I want to feel normal today," she said.

"Sure thing. Anything for you!" he said, walking over to his Mustang.

"This is a nice car. Is it new?" Katie asked as he took the top down.

"It's six months old; it's my baby," he said, smiling.

"Good choice, Brandon. This is one of my favorite cars," Katie said, getting in the car. "So what sounds good to eat?" She was ready for a nice break after a long night.

Going to a local sit-down restaurant, Brandon and Katie caught up on each other's lives.

"You know, Jacob is coming home next month. I'll ask Mark to fly down here and pick you up," Katie said.

"I would enjoy that. Thanks. I haven't seen your house since it got finished." Brandon said happily. "So about earlier, if you need to talk to someone, I'm a good listener," Brandon said, hoping she would explain the early phone call.

"I've had some issues of my own lately. I'm just trying to work through them," Katie said, trying to make some sense.

"I understand completely!" Brandon said, still worried about her. "So, it's Sunday, do you want to go golfing or something?" Brandon said, enjoying her company.

"Sure, I would like that! Katie said excitedly.

Enjoying the rest of her day, Katie went back to the beach house to take a nap.

Waking up a few hours later, Katie realized it was still daylight. Exhausted, she got up to make dinner and watch a movie. She tried to enjoy the peace and quiet, but she started to feel anxious again. Grabbing her phone, she called her mom before she left for the Bahamas the following day.

"Hey, Mom. How are you?" Katie asked, happy to hear her voice.

"How was the photo shoot?" Jackie said curiously.

"It went great. I'm just tired and bored," Katie said, tired of being lonely.

"Enjoy your break, Katie. You really need to take some time out for yourself," she said, always worried about her episodes.

"You're right. I think I'll go jogging later. That always clears my mind," Katie said.

"That's a great idea. Have fun in Florida. I love you!" her mom said, ending the call. Getting up, Katie went to get her jogging clothes on. Grabbing her iPod, Katie headed outside to do her stretches. Walking out the backdoor, Katie loved the in-ground pool fenced in with the fountains.

"Wow!" is all she could say, shocked by all Brandon's hard work.

Walking out of the fence, Katie looked down at the beach. With couples everywhere, Katie saw a man jogging alone with his dog. Seeing Katie, he stopped. With sweat all over his body, Katie was stunned by his good looks and gorgeous smile.

"Hi, neighbor," he said to her.

"Hi, but this is my vacation house," Katie said, trying to not sound rude. "I live in Missouri full time."

"Oh, I know. Brandon lives here. I have a beach house as well. I live in California full time," he said. "Brandon talks highly of you. Now I can see why. Oh, by the way, my name is Chad."

"Hi, Chad," Katie said, making complete eye contact. "My name is Katie. It's great to meet you!"

A taller man who seemed to be about six feet tall, with brown hair and blue eyes caught her attention. Chad seemed to take good care of himself in ways such as Katie did. Loving the freedom of doing what he pleased, gave him a sense of peace within himself to always work harder to be a better person. A man, not only with great looks and manners, amazed her with his deep but calming voice. Being nervous as Katie, Chad worked hard to carry an intelligent conversation. Trying to contain herself around Chad made her nervous, but as always, Katie tried to replace that feeling with a smile, something she was used to doing since she was a young child.

"Pretty evening to jog," Chad said, running out of things to say.

"Yes, I'm getting ready for my evening jog. Brandon and I went golfing all day," she said.

"That sounds like it would have been a lot of fun. Do you want a jogging partner?" he asked, staring right back at her.

"Sure, company is always nice," she said nervously. "So, California, huh?"

"Yes, San Diego, to be exact," he said to her.

"Really? My daughter lives there—in California, I mean," Katie said, smiling.

"Yeah, I work as a photographer for weddings, models, ball teams—if you name it, I do it," Chad said.

"Wow. I do that too, mainly for just models," Katie said, trying not to brag.

"Brandon showed me some of your work. Very impressive!" he said. "Ready for our run before it gets dark?"

"Sure, I'm ready whenever you are," Katie said, taking off into the sunset.

"So, I hear you're a country girl. Missouri, I think Brandon said," Chad said, smiling.

"Yes, I grew up in St. Louis, but I love the peace and quiet of the country," Katie said, knowing she loved nature that God put there for her and her family to enjoy.

"That's great. I'm happy for you. I have a beach house a few down from yours, actually," he said. "I'm here until Sunday if you want to go out sometime or a few times," he said.

"I would like that," Katie said, smiling.

"Good, me too!" Chad said, shaking her hand back at her beach house. He then walked away.

Watching him, Katie was all smiles. Going straight upstairs, Katie grabbed her cell phone to call Brandon.

"Hey, Katie. What's up?" he said.

"Hey. I met Chad, the neighbor. Is that good or bad?" Katie said, upbeat.

"Good. He's a nice guy," he said.

"Okay. I went on a jog a little bit ago with him. I just wanted to make sure he was harmless," Katie said, relieved by his answer.

"He lives in California, but he comes to his beach house on the weekends sometimes."

"Thanks for the information. He was nice, and I think we are going on a few dates this week!" she said, excited to meet a man close to her own age.

"Good for you. I'm sure you guys will get along great. You have a lot in common," Brandon said.

Excited, Katie headed downstairs to watch her movie. Walking around in a robe and house slippers, Katie heard a knock on the door. Opening the door, she was overwhelmed to see Devon and Ashley.

"Surprise!" they said, giving her a hug. "Oh my gosh!" Katie said, shocked. Following behind them was Brandon and Jacob. "You guys are going to put me in shock!" she said, amazed all her kids were there together.

"Hey, Mom. I've missed you," Jacob said, giving her a hug.

"I've missed you too—all of you. Brandon, I just talked to you a little bit ago, and you never said a word," Katie said, still trembling.

"It wouldn't be a surprise if I told you, silly!" Brandon said, knowing how much she loved and missed her kids.

"We can only stay a couple of days," Ashley said, heading up to her own room.

"I can deal with that," Katie said, thinking she was in a dream.

The rest of the night, the kids and their mom caught up on each other's lives. They all crashed out around two o'clock. Katie tossed and turned. Waking up several times, Katie couldn't believe her eyes. Now that they were all grown up, Katie finally felt a sense of relief that they

IN A STRANGER'S EYES

all took good care of themselves and were happy and healthy.

Finally, at around six o'clock, Katie decided to make breakfast for everyone. Knowing they were all tired, Katie ate and went back up to her room. Falling fast asleep, Katie was awakened by the doorbell.

"I'll get it, Mom," Devon said loud enough for her to hear her. Both shocked, Devon and Chad didn't know what to say to each other.

"Is Katie here?" Chad said, confused because she didn't say anything about company. Looking a lot like her mother, Chad began to put the pieces together.

"Come on in. I'll go let her know you are here," Devon said.

"Thanks," Chad said, as he walked into the living room and introduced himself to Katie's children. "I'll wait in the living room."

All resembling their Mom, Chad knew they had to be there as a surprise since she didn't mention them coming earlier. Jacob struck up a conversation to make the man not feel so out of place.

"Hi, my name is Jacob," Jacob said. "Nice to meet you." He was shocked to see an unknown man in his mom's living room.

"I'm Chad," Chad said, unsure of how Katie's son would react to a stranger looking for his mother. "It's nice to meet you too."

"Mom, are you ready for this?" Devon asked her.

"Ready for what, honey?" Katie asked, just sleeping well finally after a long night.

"There's a man downstairs asking for you," her daughter said to her, trying to catch her attention.

"What does he look like?" Katie said, looking a mess.

"Well, I'd say six feet three inches, two hundred pounds, blue eyes, brown hair—is any of this ringing a bell?" Devon said, excited for her mom.

"Chad is here this early?" Katie said, scrambling around to find nice clothes and get ready.

"It's not early; it's noon, Mother," she said, knowing her mom had been a sleepwalker her whole life.

"Did you see the note I left about breakfast?' Katie said, trying to catch her breath.

"Yes, it was great, but we wanted you to get some sleep. It's Monday—your first official day of vacation," Devon said.

"Thanks. I feel better," Katie said, kissing her on the forehead. "I still can't believe you are all here; what a huge surprise!" Katie said, trying not to cry.

"We had it all planned for the past month," Ashley said, walking through the door and surprising them both.

"I know, and I just saw you the other day at my house," Katie said, giving Ashley a hug and a kiss. "What's Jacob doing?"

"Talking to a hot guy waiting patiently for you to come downstairs!" Devon said, trying not to laugh.

"I'm getting ready as fast as I can, girls. I look like a mess," Katie said, trying to contain herself.

"You look fine, Mother," Ashley said.

"Thanks, honey. Let's do this!" Katie said nervously. Walking down the stairs with a pair of khaki capris and a brown tank top, Katie always wore flip flops to feel more comfortable. Having her hair half way up, Katie's features stood out even more.

As Katie walked downstairs, Chad looked up, amazed at how different she looked out of her jogging clothes.

"Hey, Chad. Nice surprise," is all she could say.

"Yes, I thought I'd see if all of you and Brandon wanted to go out on my yacht. The weather is perfect," Chad said, hoping she would say yes.

"That would be great. Everyone else in?" Katie asked, knowing they would enjoy it as well.

"Yes, I'll call Brandon," Jacob said, heading into the kitchen.

"Okay, I live three houses down, if you guys want to meet me there in two hours," Chad said, heading back to the front door.

"Okay. We will see you then," Katie said, trying to keep from making eye contact.

"Sounds good, and nice meeting all of you," Chad said, closing the door behind him.

"Mom, he's so good for you!" Devon said, knowing her mom didn't date much since her and her father split up when she was eleven.

"I like him. We went jogging last night, and I was impressed," Katie said, grabbing a bite to eat.

"Brandon will be here in the next hour," Jacob said.

"Great! Family day; how exciting!" Katie said, thrilled. "Thanks so much, everyone. You have no idea what this means to me," she said, starting to get emotional.

"We do know. It means just as much to us too, Mom," Ashley said, still worried about her health. Filling Jacob, Devon, and Brandon in on her condition, it better prepared them to deal with it if it were to happen while they were there.

"What are we going to do until we leave to go?" Jacob said, knowing he couldn't be out flirting on the beach.

"I don't know, but where is your girlfriend?" Katie asked, forgetting to ask earlier.

"She's still on tour. I had taken these days off a month ago, before I met her," he said, knowing he finally met the woman for him.

"And you, Devon, is there anyone I should know about?" Katie asked, drilling all her kids.

"No, Mom. I'm too busy with work to have a serious relationship," Devon said.

"Okay, Ashley, what about you? You live three miles away, and you never mention a boyfriend either," Katie said, hoping her daughters would find true love.

"I'm not ready yet either. I work two jobs and go to college—that keeps me way too busy for a relationship," Ashley told her.

Knowing how her mom and dad fought for so many years, Katie always stayed away from the dating scene as much as possible. "I've been there, honey. You have seen me work two jobs, go to college, and raise you on my own," Katie said, heading back to her room.

"Okay, we are going to the beach to lay out for a little bit," they said, grabbing their swim clothes.

"Love you guys! Have fun!" Katie said, still exhausted from the night before.

Walking into her room and closing the door behind her for privacy, Katie stopped and saw a young man's face. He was seventeen years old and short, with a small frame. Katie would be shocked at the trouble he would get himself into. Living several states away, the boy would drive his new car his parents bought for him for his birthday and outrun several cops in many states. Finally catching him, the joyride would come to a complete halt as fast as he hit the spikes on the highway. Looking only twelve years old, Katie wondered what was going through his mind, not thinking there would be consequences for his actions.

"Mom, Brandon is here," Jacob said from the bottom of the staircase.

"Okay. I'll be there in a little bit!" Katie said, rocking back and forth, trying to get that image out of her mind. Slowly getting up, Katie went to the bathroom to splash cold water on her face. Knowing she needed another shower from all the sweat, Katie grabbed some clothes real fast and hurried to gather herself back to her normal, upbeat personality.

"Time to go, Mom. Are you about ready?" Ashley said, knowing they only had fifteen minutes left before they had to be at Chad's house.

"I'm on my way!" Katie said all ready for her day in the sun.

"Thank goodness. What took you so long? We were getting worried," Jacob said, forgetting about what Ashley had told them on the limousine ride to the beach house.

"Sorry. I get a little distracted from time to time," is all she could think to say.

"That's all right; no worries. I was kidding. No big deal, really," Jacob said, trying to catch himself.

"Okay, gang. Let's go have some fun. What do you say?" Katie said, grabbing her purse.

"Yes, it will be a blast, and maybe you will have a boyfriend by the end of the day," Devon said, smiling, trying to make her mood brighter.

CHAPTER 4

Heading out to Chad's yacht, Katie couldn't believe her eyes. Even with the money she had worked so hard for, Katie had never been on a yacht before; taking on yet another learning experience, Katie was thrilled to enjoy the day with her family first and foremost.

"Wow, Chad, this is beautiful! I'm impressed!" Katie said, still shocked by the size.

"Thanks. I enjoy it when I come here," Chad said, showing everyone how to board his yacht.

Floating out into the ocean with clear skies as far as she could see, Katie picked a seat and enjoyed the rays. With her kids carrying conversations back and forth, Chad came over and sat by Katie to break the ice a little more.

"So, Katie, thanks for spending the day with me," Chad said, smiling. "It gets pretty boring out here alone."

"Thanks for the invite, Chad," Katie said, feeling the chemistry getting stronger as she talked to Chad one-on-

one in such a beautiful place. "It was a great surprise for all of us. I wasn't expecting my kids to surprise me, so this week has started out wonderful!"

As the day seemed to fly by, Chad moved around different islands that he was familiar with. Docking on a big island that seemed deserted, Chad pulled out a lot of food—fried chicken, cole slaw, and potato salad.

"I thought we all might get hungry so I packed us plenty of food," Chad said, heading to a picnic table near the shade. "Is everyone in?"

Chad led the pack; Katie and her kids followed behind him.

"This is usually very busy," Chad said. "It's still pretty early, so we can have a peaceful meal and then head back to beach house. It's been a great, relaxing day. Thanks to everyone for coming out; you all seem like very down to earth people."

Spending the day and part of the evening out on the water, everyone enjoyed the calm waves of the ocean. Docking the yacht back, Katie grabbed her things and led the group to the car.

"Thanks, Chad, for everything. That was so much fun!" Katie said as Brandon and her kids loaded up.

"Thanks for coming. I enjoyed all your company," Chad said, walking away.

"Hey, do you want to do lunch tomorrow? My kids are flying out at noon. After I get back, I'm free the rest of the day," she said, amazed at the chemistry they both shared.

IN A STRANGER'S EYES

"Sure. Here's my cell phone number. Just give me a call anytime," he said, walking toward her.

"Thanks. I'll talk to you later," Katie said, getting in the front seat of Brandon's car.

Exhausted, they went back to Katie's beach house to take showers. "Who's up for dinner and a club?" Jacob asked as they all stopped. "It's our last night here!"

"Sure, let's do it!" Katie said, grabbing her phone to call Brandon and Chad to invite them as well.

"Meet downstairs in an hour. Does that sound good?" Jacob said, knowing they always took extra time to get ready.

"Okay, it will be fun. Brandon and Chad can show us around," Katie said, walking into her room, gently closing the bedroom door behind her.

Making arrangements with Brandon and Chad, Katie could hardly contain herself. Looking through her clothes, Katie had trouble finding something appropriate to wear. Always a blue jeans and T-shirt kind of woman, Katie usually only dressed up for work. Knowing Devon and Ashley were about the same size as her, Katie went to their room, trying to look great for their her date with Chad.

"Mom, you always look good no matter what you wear," Ashley said.

"Thanks. I think I'm just going out in casual clothes," Katie said, trying to get their opinion.

"We are just wearing slacks, a nice shirt, and shoes, just in case. We don't want to be underdressed," Devon said, always a fashion icon growing up.

"Yes, I don't want to draw too much attention in a strange place," Ashley said, getting ready for her shower.

With all three ladies dressed in black slacks, nice shirt and shoes, the men downstairs were in awe—not used to seeing them all dressed up for a night out on the town. Devon, with long brown hair to her waist and standing about five-foot-three, and blue eyes, a trait she inherited from her father. Devon kept herself in shape because she was a choreographer in California. Ashley, a spitting image of Katie was blessed with more height, standing five-foot-seven and slim. Ashley had blonde hair, shoulder length, and hazel eyes. With both of her daughters having high cheekbones like their Mother, they all resembled each other so much.

"Ladies, you look beautiful!" Brandon said, watching them come downstairs.

"Thanks, Brandon. Let's go have some more fun. I think we are all starving," Katie said, smiling at Chad. Always modest, Katie learned not to be persistent when it came to men. From getting too much negative attention from Mike to never trusting a man, Katie tried to get close but then always found an excuse to be alone.

"Your kids and I will ride in my car; you and Chad can take your his truck, if that works for you," Brandon said, trying to play matchmaker.

"Sure, sounds good to me," Chad said, opening her door.

"Thanks," is all she could say, trying to be her normal, happy self.

"Do I make you nervous?" Chad asked, curious by her facial expressions from time to time.

"No, not at all. I'm a little shy sometimes," she said, trying not to sound pathetic.

"Oh, that makes me feel better," Chad said, relieved by her answer. "I think we have a lot in common, other than you're a country girl and I'm a city boy," he said, trying to make her laugh.

"Whatever. I will always have some city in me," Katie said, smiling. "I wish you didn't live so many states away," Katie said, trying to get more comfortable around him.

"Well, I have a jet, and so do you. It's only a few hours each way, or for the first couple of months, we can meet at my beach house every other weekend or something. I would hate to kick Brandon out all the time," Chad said, liking that idea already.

"Yeah, I think that would be a great idea!" Katie said.

"Well, here we are, Miss Katie," he said, following Brandon to the steak house.

"Why does everyone keep calling me Miss Katie?" Katie asked, curious.

"It's because you are very nice and respectful to everyone," Chad said, looking into her eyes. "It's a form of respect. It means I like you!"

After dinner, they all went over to a club across the street. With the music loud, she couldn't remember the last time she was in a place this full.

"Nice club. Good choice, Brandon," Jacob said.

"Wait, you have a girlfriend," Ashley said, knowing her brother was quite the player in his early twenties.

"No worries. I'm a grown man, and I know what I have waiting for me tomorrow," Jacob said.

"Okay, I can tell you have changed for the better, and I'm proud of you for that," Ashley said, giving him a hug.

"Thanks. I have come a long way, huh?" Jacob said, trying to be macho.

"I'm feeling old," Katie said to Brandon and Chad while trying to make it to an empty table.

"I heard you were in a music video. A dancer, in fact," Brandon said, trying to break her hard shell.

"Really? That's exciting!" Chad said, not really surprised.

"Yes, but that was a long time ago. Give me time, and I will be out there dancing," Katie said, knowing she loved to dance her whole life, from ballet to hip hop.

Chad, a man in his mid forties always attracted women from his good looks to his great personality. He always seemed to light up a room with just his smile.

"So, how old are you while we are telling little secrets?" Katie said to Chad.

"I'm forty-three, and yourself?" Chad said.

"Forty-five. Feel better?" Katie said, teasing him.

"Yes, that does, actually. You have so many things going for you. Why on earth are you single? Do you have a crazy side or something?" Chad said, not having any clue about her condition. It got quiet all of a sudden. Brandon asked Chad to help him get the drinks.

"Katie, what do you want to drink?" he asked as she sat there, not saying anything.

"Water for me," she said, wondering if her episodes would classify her as crazy.

Feeling really bad, Brandon explained to Chad about the things her children informed him of only a day earlier.

"What should I say to her to fix this, Brandon?" Chad said, wondering if he had already blown his chance with Katie. Feeling a strong connection with her already, Chad wanted things to keep flowing in a positive way.

"Chad, calm down," Brandon said, making Chad feel a little better already. "This isn't your fault. It will fix itself. She's a very strong, understanding woman. You didn't know; it's not your fault."

Brandon hoped Devon and Ashley would put Katie in a better mood.

"Did I say something wrong? I would never think you would have a crazy side. Look at your life and all you have," Chad said.

Walking back to their table with their drinks in their hands, Brandon and Chad approached Katie with big smiles on their faces, hoping Katie didn't catch the whole conversation before they left. With Katie sitting at her table waiting for their return, Chad and Brandon tried to change the subject.

"So, Katie how long have you lived in Missouri?" Chad said.

"My whole life," Katie said. "I like it there. The weather is unpredictable at times, but other than that, it's a nice state."

With Katie still remembering the statement Chad made, she tried to ignore the way it made her feel.

"Did I say something wrong earlier?" Chad asked, trying not to make the situation worse. "I would never think that way of you. We all have issues to deal with in our lives. I think you are a very bright, talented woman!"

"Thanks, Chad," Katie said, letting the awkward conversation flow away while she enjoyed her vacation with her kids. "I'm very blessed with everything I have been given. Brandon, will you please take me back to the beach house and come back after the kids?"

"Katie, your kids will be upset if you leave. Remember, they leave tomorrow at noon," Brandon said, hoping she would change her mind.

"You're right, I don't want to leave," Katie said, putting it all out on the table. "Chad, I have an issue that's not really crazy. It's just sometimes I see things in my mind that scares me and others that are around at that time."

"I understand. You are a wonderful, beautiful woman and very smart. I like everything about you!" Chad said, grateful she opened up, even if in a crowded place.

"Thanks. I feel the same way about you. Now it's my turn. Are you hiding a wife in California?" Katie said, trying to get her sense of humor back.

"No wife—or kids, for that matter," Chad said. "My wife passed away from cancer ten years ago, and I never found anyone like you—until now."

"Oh, Chad, I'm so sorry!" Katie said, feeling very small at that exact moment.

"We are all thrown difficult tasks in our own lives; that was mine and Brandon's," Chad said, hoping Brandon couldn't hear him over the loud music.

"You're right. I have been through more things than most people ever have to deal with in their lifetime, and I think that's the way I am, really," Katie said.

Growing up in what most people thought was a fairy tale family, Katie had suffered many trying times. Katie had been sexually abused by someone close to her behind a closed door. Nobody knew about it except for her, until she was in her twenties. Katie had broken down and told a close friend what had happened to her. Thinking that the closure would help, Katie went on to move out of a nice subdivision in the city to a small trailer with her mom and sisters. As the walls of Katie's life had slowly crumbled around her, she had witnessed the life that she had only heard about on the news. She had seen drugs being dealt next door to her. One of her neighbor's children, at the age of eleven, had been locked out of the refrigerator and locked in her room while her parents and other siblings had eaten, drunk beer, and partied like the young girl didn't exist. Then one day she had locked herself in the bathroom and taken a bottle of Aspirin, hoping and praying God would take her to a safer place away from the nightmare she lived up until that day. Remembering the parents celebrating the young child's death, Katie wondered how people could be so heartless to another human being. Trying to conquer her own life day by day, Katie had tried to keep herself grounded and strong enough to stay away from the crowds that liked to get high, pop pills, and drink on a daily basis, as if it was the best way to live. Staying to herself most of the time, Katie had watched her own family try to survive on what little income was there. Living had seemed normal when she was a child. Katie had been set free from the abuse long enough to meet someone else that had swept her off her feet at the age of twenty one. What seemed perfect then, only would change when everyone was faced different directions. Used to the abuse, Katie had forgiven time and time again the man who had fathered her three children, until she stood up to the plate. She had finished her education ten years after dropping out of high school, thinking a job would help her family more. Becoming an independent woman, Katie had worked in law enforcement for fifteen years, helping others that were dealing with abuse as well. Trying to raise her kids and work twelve hour shifts, Katie had learned to multi-task well beyond her years. Always wanting to be a model, Katie had gone to an audition and had been picked from several others to follow her dreams at the age of twenty four. Always putting her kids first, Katie had enjoyed the time she had had to herself, getting picked in several movies roles and learning the wardrobe, make up, and hair as well in her time off work. With paving her way to a future she only could dream of, Katie had jumped many hurdles, making a choice when her kids were in their late teenage years to resign her duties in law enforcement and find another place where she could belong and still raise her kids that suffered many medical issues including bipolar disorder. Never judging anyone for their flaws,

Katie stood behind her family first and watched the rest fall into place.

"I like the way you are. We are both hardheaded and independent," Chad said, laughing.

"Yes, that fits me for sure," Katie said, turning to watch her kids on the dance floor. "I'm so glad they came to stay a couple of days. I missed them terribly. It's been a while since we were in the same house this long. Holidays seem to fly by," Katie said, leaning over to put her head on his shoulder.

"You're a great mom. They are lucky to have you, Katie; I'm sure you know that," Chad said.

"My children grew up with a man that treated them like they had no feelings because they were young," Katie said, hoping he would understand since he had grown up an only child. "No matter my way of thinking, it would always clash with Mike, that's their dad's name. He loves his kids, just in a different way, I guess would be easier to explain. He grew up in a family that was full of abuse a lot like mine, but with drugs and the drinking on top of all that. Having a family with me, he would never let go of his past, which made him want to treat his kids the same way. I would debate his beliefs until I realized I couldn't change his mind, then when I watched my children begin to react to his behavior, I did what I thought would change them from following the same foot steps as him. It wasn't easy, but after several years, they began to calm down and saw what a life without drama was. One of my many accomplishments as a single mother."

"Job well done!" he said, smiling, showing his dimples.

"Hey, Mom! Are you guys coming out to dance?" Devon asked, hoping she would have some fun.

"No, Chad and I are talking. You guys have fun!" Katie said, knowing they would understand. Brandon joined all of the kids, while Chad and Katie got to know each other better.

"Thanks, Chad," Katie said. "I count my blessings every day still. Even though my kids have a sense of direction now, that is always subject to change. I just hope for the best and prepare myself for the worst."

Katie remembered all of their trying times fighting peer pressure and walking away, which rarely happened with Jacob.

"So, not to change the subject, but what do you want to do tomorrow?" he asked, hoping she wanted to do something spontaneous again. "You know, I have a Harley-Davidson motorcycle, if you like that that kind of thing. You don't look like the biker-type girl; though, I could be wrong."

"Well, you don't look like the biker type either," Katie said.

"No, but that's what makes us both unique. So, are you a biker girl?" he asked curiously.

"Yes, it's very relaxing," Katie said, feeling more comfortable around him already.

"Then that's what we will do," he said, liking her a lot already.

"Last call!" the DJ said, ending the night with a slow song.

"Do you want to dance?" Chad asked.

"Sure!" Katie said, excited.

Hearing a slow song come on, Katie walked with Chad to the dance floor. Hand in hand, Chad spun Katie around to him, making her very close to his big, broad chest. Looking around, Katie saw her kids and Chad on the sidelines as Ashley and Devon were crying tears of joy for their Mom. Smelling his Polo, Katie couldn't help but wonder how she got so lucky meeting the man of her dreams in Florida where she least expected it. Dancing to the entire dance, Katie felt her nose touch Chad's cheek. Shocked to be that close to a man, Katie thanked him for the dance and walked away, leaving Chad speechless.

"It's really loud in here; do you want to take a walk with me outside, so we can talk more?" Chad asked, not wanting to make her feel uncomfortable.

"Sure, I would like that. Besides, it's a nice night out," Katie said, grinning from ear to ear.

Taking a stroll down to the beach, Katie and Chad held hands as if they were two teenagers in love.

"You know, Katie, I'm so happy to finally meet you," Chad said. "Never did I think I would have feelings for you!"

"I feel the same way, Chad. It's a great feeling, something I haven't felt ever," Katie said, as they came close enough to kiss.

"Mom, Chad, bars closed. We will meet you back at the house!" Jacob said, happy for his Mom.

Happy for the distraction since she had just met Chad, Katie said, "I think I'm ready to head back to the house, are you?" She was relieved nothing had happened.

"Sure, whenever you are," Chad said, following her back to his truck.

Going back to the beach house, Chad and Katie were quiet.

"Is something wrong?" Chad asked Katie.

"No, I'm just exhausted. Thanks for today," Katie said, just wanting some sleep.

"Me too. You're here. Tomorrow, call me, and we can take a ride, if you still want," Chad said.

"Sure! I would love that!" Katie said, feeling reassured that he knew about her problem.

Meeting Brandon and her kids inside, they all had big smiles on their faces.

"What?" Katie asked, knowing why they were all smiling.

"You know what, and we are happy to see you smiling again," Jacob said, remembering watching his mom cry herself to sleep every night for many years.

"You deserve this, Mom. We will all leave at ease, knowing Chad and Brandon will keep you company," Devon said, hugging her mom.

"And you know, since Devon and I will be in California, you can visit Chad then too," Ashley said knowing she wanted to help her mom on the photography business but, at the same time, wanted to further her career.

"I understand, Ashley. I was young once, and I think you're making the right choice, and all of you, while you're here, are always welcome to come and work at either business," Katie told them, trying not to cry.

"Mom, we are proud of you. We always have been!" they said, all giving her a hug.

"We all have to live out our dreams, just like you do every day, and before we get too old, we will be working right alongside you at your house. We respect your support on letting us do what makes us happy," Jacob said.

"We are and always have been a great team, and thanks to all of you for spending a couple of days with me. You don't know how happy that makes me!" Katie said.

"Mom, we are going to bed. It's been a long day on the water and then dinner and dancing. We will get up early and make breakfast for you, just like you did for us!" Ashley said, watching everyone go to their own rooms for some much-needed sleep.

"Hey, Brandon. You can stay, if you want, and eat breakfast and hang out; it would mean a lot to all of us!" Katie said, putting a smile on his face.

"Thanks. It means a lot to me too," he said, grabbing some blankets for the couch.

"Good night, Katie," he said, so happy to see her with her three kids.

"Good night, Brandon. You have a family here with us; we will always be just a phone call away, okay?" Katie said.

"You have and always will be one of my many angels, along with your family," Brandon said, trying not to cry. "Good night, Katie. See you in the morning."

"Right back at you!" Katie said, winking at him with a smile.

Washing her face and getting dressed for bed, Katie didn't even think before she fell fast asleep.

Sleeping so well, Katie couldn't believe everyone was awake and cooking downstairs. Looking at the time on her phone, she was shocked it was already 9:30 a.m.

Oh my gosh, Katie thought, rushing to get ready.

"Mom, breakfast is ready!" Ashley said, walking into her room. Hearing the shower, she knocked on the bathroom door. "Mom, time to eat when you are done," she said.

"Thanks, honey. I'll be down soon," Katie said, trying to hurry, knowing her kids were leaving at noon.

"Okay. Love you," Ashley said, heading back downstairs.

"Me too, and thanks!" Katie said, getting ready to look nice for her last meal with her kids before they boarded their plane to go back to work and what they now called "home." Doing her hair and makeup really fast, Katie put on jeans, a nice shirt, and tennis shoes—the clothes that made her feel most comfortable.

Heading downstairs, she heard the kitchen get quiet.

"Hello?" Katie said.

"Surprise!" Katie heard from everyone. Shocked, she saw her dad, Glen; stepmom, Hannah; and Grandma Dee, who recently turned one hundred years old, as well as Rachel, Casey, and their families.

Shocked by the surprise, Katie put her hands over her mouth, trying not to cry. "Mom, we thought we would all surprise you here since this is your vacation!" Devon said, giving her Mother a hug.

Still in awe, Katie gave everyone hugs. "What is this all for? I don't understand," Katie said.

"Well, one thing, Jackie, your mom, is in the Bahamas with Sam. That is why they are not here," Ashley said, trying to get a word in.

"We know how much your family means to you, and you mean the world to us too. It's all our vacation, so we wanted to do this as a small token of our appreciation for all you do for us!" Casey said.

"Thanks, but without all of you, everything we have wouldn't be possible," Katie said, confused.

"It's your dedication that keeps all of us going, and we are all leaving at noon. This was a last minute thing, but we knew you would be happy to see everyone!" Casey said as she saw Katie still trying to control her emotions.

"You're welcome. Now let's eat and relax by the pool," Ashley said, smiling.

"Hey, Katie. You don't mind me being here, do you?" Brandon said, feeling a little out of place.

"No, you are part of our family. Please stay!" Katie said. Enjoying their time together, Katie hung out with everyone until it was time for them to leave.

With everyone cleaning up their messes, Katie got out her camera for some family photos. "Just because I still can't believe you are all here, please get together, and let me cherish this forever."

"Mom, we still need to pack, so let us go first," her kids said, getting in front of everyone else.

"Okay. It will only take a few minutes," Katie said, knowing she was going to miss them when they were all gone.

Hearing the doorbell, Katie went to answer the door. "Hey, Chad! Come on in!" Katie said, happy to see him. "Give me a few minutes to take some pictures, and I will introduce you to everyone before they leave!"

"Sure, no problem, but if you want, I'll take one of you and your kids," he said.

"Thanks, and yes!" Katie said, giving him the camera.

After all the pictures were done, Katie took him around to meet her family. "The only one not here is my mother and stepfather. They left for the Bahamas on Monday."

"We have to load up everybody so we don't miss our plane," Jacob said with his bag in hand. Giving everyone hugs and kisses, Katie watched them all load up in the limousine.

"Bye! Thanks, and I love you!" Katie said, waving good-bye to everyone, including her kids and family, as they departed from her beach house with Brandon. Holding her hand up to keep the sun from shining in her eyes, Katie was still shocked to see everyone show up there to surprise her. Looking the opposite direction, Katie saw Chad sitting on his Harley. Smiling, she walked over to him—excited for a nice, relaxing day.

"So, do you still want to go for a ride?" Chad asked in his blue jeans and T-shirt.

"Sure, let me go change and put my hair up," Katie said, feeling like a normal person again.

"Okay. I'll meet you outside," he said, smiling, showing his dimples.

"Okay," she said, excited about spending the day with Chad.

Going to her room, Katie threw her hair up and changed her shirt. Walking back downstairs, Katie still was in shock to see her family. Her grandma Dee was always like her best friend. Living with her dad and stepmother, Katie tried to hang out with her as much as possible. Even at her age, she was able to get around and have a sharp mind.

Walking outside, Katie saw Chad standing by his motorcycle.

"Hey, Chad, are you ready for a great day on your motorcycle?" Katie said, knowing she was.

Loving the outdoors, Katie remembered back to a time in her life she had friends that would take her to Illinois just to relax and take pictures. She had known then in her early thirties that the simple things in life are what would matter the most.

"Yes, I'm ready whenever you are," Chad said as Katie climbed on the bike with him. "Oh, and Katie, thanks for being the spontaneous woman that you are. I like to do things unexpected from time to time."

Riding the rest of the day, they took many stops for Katie to take pictures. "So, when are you heading back to the country?" Chad said, staring at her.

"Sunday. I have to get back to work on Monday," she said, looking at him out of the corner of her eye.

"That's good. We can hang out and enjoy each other's company, if that works for you, of course," Chad said.

"Of course. I would like that," Katie said, still overwhelmed with everything that happened that morning.

"You have a nice family. You should be grateful, which I'm sure you are," he said, knowing how close they all were.

"Yes, I am. They are my everything," she said.

"So, is there room for a boyfriend?" Chad said nervously.

"Yes, I think there is," Katie said, putting her helmet back on.

Smiling, they both knew there was a spark that kept getting brighter as they talked. Riding back to her beach house, Chad decided to surprise Katie and stop at a restaurant near the ocean to have a romantic meal and watch the sunset.

"Wow, this is beautiful Chad!" Katie said as she climbed off the back of his bike. Watching the boats, jet skis, and yachts dock, Katie could see people from many different angles coming in for the night.

"I thought you would like it. This is one of my favorite places to just come and think," he said to her, smiling and showing his big dimples.

"I can see why, very relaxing, I think we are going to get along just fine," Katie said, walking past him to head closer to the shore.

"You are full of surprises. I like that!" Katie said, not wanting to fall too fast, knowing he lived all the way in California.

"Thanks. That, I am, but only good ones. No worries," Chad said.

"So, you know my life story. What about you?" Katie said, trying not to upset him.

"Well, it's simple, really. I was adopted at age three by a nice couple that couldn't have kids of their own. I never met my biological family. I married my high school sweetheart, and I told you about what happened to her. That pretty much sums me up," he said in one long breath.

"Wow, mine would take a few hours," Katie said chuckling.

"Yes, but that's interesting. Mine is an open book; yours has mystery to it," Chad said, trying to make her laugh.

"Mine is interesting, to say the least," Katie said, not even knowing where to start.

"No worries. We can do yours another day," he said, knowing she suffered a lot of things in her past.

"Thanks. Yeah, it's a long story all the way through, and I'm only forty-five," Katie said, looking at the menu. "I have to go to the ladies room; I'll be right back."

Walking to the bathroom, Katie looked back, still amazed she could attract a man like Chad, a man that knew how to respect everyone no matter the situation. Walking into the stall, Katie shut the door behind her. Feeling her head start to spin, Katie sat down on the floor. Rocking back in forth, Katie saw a scary man's face with long, black hair and cold, blue eyes. Katie started to shake. A man in his late forties would stab two men in a bar parking lot and spend over half of his life in prison. Full of tattoos and piercings, Katie couldn't get his face out of her head.

"Ma'am, should I call nine-one-one?" a woman said, trying to get her up off the floor. With her eyes fully dilated and wide open, she didn't know what else to do.

"Someone call an ambulance now!" she said, watching her breathing go fast and then very slow.

With all the excitement going on, Chad saw many people run to the restroom. *Katie!* he thought, following the crowd.

"It's okay. No need to call nine-one-one. She has episodes. Get some cold water, please," Chad said, trying to wake her up. "Katie, it's me, Chad. Please wake up!"

Putting cold water on her face, Katie blinked her eyes and saw Chad and a big crowd of strangers looking at her.

"Are you all right?" Chad said, scared.

"Yeah. What happened?" Katie said to him.

"I don't know. I guess you had a spell," he said, helping her up.

"Sorry for the scare, everyone. I'm okay," she said, heading for the sink.

As everyone cleared out, Chad stepped out to give her privacy. After fixing her hair, Katie walked outside, feeling ashamed.

"You scared me for a few minutes," Chad said, still shaken up.

"I'm sorry. I never know when they come. It just happens," Katie said, hoping it wouldn't scare him off.

"I'm just glad you're all right ," Chad said hugging her.

"Thanks, and I am truly sorry," Katie told him.

"Do you still want to eat?" he asked, knowing she had traumatizing things happen.

"Yeah, but all of these people are staring at us," Katie said, embarrassed.

"That's okay; they were just worried, like me," he said, making her feel better.

On the ride back to her beach house, Katie just enjoyed the fresh air. "You're back, safe and sound. Do you want to come to my house? I will sleep on the couch," Chad said, scared to leave her alone.

"Thanks. I would like that," Katie said, getting off his motorcycle to grab some clothes. "I need to change. Do you mind waiting for me?" she said with a smile.

"No, that's fine," he said, following her inside. Walking upstairs, Katie hurried to take a shower, hoping she wouldn't have to see that scary man's face ever again.

Walking downstairs in her nightclothes and wet hair, Chad couldn't believe how nice she looked without makeup. "Okay. I'm ready," Katie said, excited to have company again.

"All right, let's go. I need a shower too," Chad said, knowing he was close to his house. Walking into his house, Katie looked around at how clean and organized he kept his house. With only the simple furniture, Chad only came there when he needed a break from his house in California. A widowed man, Chad liked everything simple—just how Katie liked it.

"I like your house," Katie said. "It's nice. How long have you had this?"

"Five years. After my wife passed away, I wanted a place to get away from my work," he said, trying not to sound too boring. "I bought my yacht as a present to myself and take it out only a few times a year. It gets lonely sometimes by myself," Chad said, knowing she knew how he felt.

"I know the feeling. I'm happy my family lives on my property, but they all have their own lives, so I try not to bother them," Katie said, knowing she was so blessed to have such great, positive people surrounding her.

"Here's where you can sleep," he said as he grabbed clothes out of his dresser to take a shower.

"Okay, thanks. Are you sure I can take your bed? I can sleep on the couch," Katie said, feeling as if she were putting him out.

"No, I wouldn't think of it. I have other rooms but not much furniture, since nobody stays here usually but me," he said, happy she was staying. "If you're not tired yet, I have a huge TV downstairs. We can watch a movie, unless you want to go to sleep; it has been a long day."

"No, I'm going to try to get some sleep, and just a heads-up, I'm a sleepwalker," Katie said, throwing a little bit more on his plate.

"Really? Then maybe you should sleep on the couch so you don't fall down the stairs," he said.

"Or I can walk home and sleep. I've sleepwalked my whole life and never fell down any stairs yet," Katie said, grabbing her things and walking downstairs. Not used to sleeping in anyone else's house but her own, Katie decided to change her mind about staying at his house.

Teasing her about being so sensitive, Chad was hoping she would change her mind and stay with him.

"Katie, you don't have to leave; I was kidding," he said, not knowing she was so sensitive.

"Thanks for the offer, but I don't think you can deal with my issues," Katie said, walking outside to walk back to her beach house.

"Katie, I'm sorry. You take things way too personal," he said, making the situation worse.

Not paying attention to him, Katie went to her beach house and up to her room to go to sleep. Upset by his comments, Katie lay on her bed and cried. She finally fell asleep. Katie awoke to her cell phone going off. Her text from Chad said:

> Katie, I don't want to put any pressure on you at all, I like you a lot, and I hope you feel the same way about me. I know we just met, and I don't want to rush anything either, just one day at a time!

The next morning, Katie went to make some breakfast and get ready for a morning jog. Stretching, Katie went out the backdoor, only to find Chad sleeping on her lawn chair.

"Chad, what are you doing here?" Katie asked, shocked.

"I wanted to talk to you, and I thought this would catch your attention," he said, sounding desperate.

"Chad, I don't know why you are even here, maybe we just weren't meant to be," Katie said, trying to hold back her tears. "You need to leave before I call the cops. You are a jerk, and I don't want to see you again!"

"Fine. If that's what you wish, I will leave. It was nice meeting you, Katie," Chad said, kissing her hand.

"I knew you were too good to be true," Katie said, getting ready to take off on the beach. Looking back as Chad headed towards his house, Katie was unsure if she had made the right choice in scaring him away. Hurt by so many men in her lifetime, Katie wasn't sure if she was ready to put her heart into someone that wasn't completely comfortable with the way she was with all of her problems that were far beyond her control. Disappointed, she decided to call Brandon to take her to the airport and go home early.

"Why? What's the matter?" Brandon asked, concerned.

"I have a lot to get done for next week, and I had a good time here," Katie said.

"What about Chad, if you don't mind me asking?" he said, knowing he made her happy.

"He's rude, and I'll tell you about it another time, okay?" Katie said, putting her phone away.

Coming back from her jog, Katie saw Chad outside of his beach house staring at her. Getting out her phone again, Katie called Brandon to stay with her until she was ready to leave.

"Sure. Be there in about thirty minutes," Brandon said, knowing something bad had to have happened.

"Okay. Please hurry!" Katie said as she went upstairs to pack.

Hearing the doorbell, Katie went to see who it was. Looking through the peephole, she saw Chad.

"Katie, please talk to me. I feel horrible. I meant no disrespect, really. It just came out wrong," Chad said, pleading for her forgiveness.

Opening the door, Katie knew she was overreacting. "I'm leaving to go back home; I have a lot to do. I'm not used to having a man around. I'm truly sorry, but if you can't deal with my issues now, we are wasting each other's time."

"Knock, knock," Brandon said, coming in the front door.

"I'll be ready in a few minutes; I'm almost packed," Katie said, knowing she didn't want to go home to a quiet house again.

"Katie, I'm not going to beg anymore. I will respect your wishes and leave," Chad said, walking out her front door.

"Do I even want to know?" Brandon said, watching her wipe tears from her eyes.

"Brandon, this may sound juvenile, but he makes fun of things I do like sleepwalking," Katie asked, trying not to cry. "Am I overreacting?"

"Katie, yes, you are overreacting," Brandon said, knowing Katie was throwing away somebody that was meant for her in every way. "You're putting too much thought and energy into this and getting nothing but negative out of it. Chad knows all about you—the good, bad, and unthinkable. He accepts that. You should just humor him sometimes and not be so serious all of the time!"

"You're right, Brandon," Katie said, giving him a much needed hug. "Thank you for this talk. I was getting so upset over nothing!"

"Yes, but that is forgivable," Brandon said, knowing Chad made her really happy. "Don't throw away a good man because he said something not knowing he would hurt your feelings. See, then you both lose."

"I'm confused. I really like him. What should I do?" Katie said, sitting on her couch.

"Fix it before it's too late," Brandon said, sitting next to her.

"You're right. I have no patience; he's perfect for me," Katie said, running to the front door to see if Chad was still walking back to his beach house.

"Chad!" she yelled, hoping he was just in his backyard.

"Yes, I'm right here," he said, startling her.

"Wow, I didn't know you were still here," Katie said, trying to figure out a way to apologize again for her behavior. " I'm glad that you are though. I don't know how to do this whole relationship thing. I haven't been in one for many years."

Katie looked into his eyes.

"Katie, it's all about trust; without that, we are wasting each other's time," Chad said, knowing he was nervous about having feelings for a woman after being a widow for five years and never dreaming of his life with another woman besides his wife until now.

"I know, and I do trust you," Katie said, knowing his feelings were the same. "I think I'm just confused as to what is real with us. I mean, we just met a few days ago, and I already like you a lot!"

"Don't be afraid because I won't hurt you," Chad said, hoping she would trust him enough to get past the hardest part, what they were going through now. "I promise. I know that you have heard that from other guys in your past, but I'm not them. I'm different. Please allow me to prove that to you one day at a time."

"I understand what you are saying, Chad," Katie said, knowing he would understand. "I do trust you. I just need to learn to trust out relationship. I'm sorry, Chad, for everything that hasn't been perfect!"

"Katie, please listen to me when I came here for my vacation, I never knew I was going to meet you and have such a strong chemistry, so I understand it is scary, but I'm willing to take the chance if you are," Chad said, hoping she would agree.

"I know," Katie said, as tears began to flow down her cheeks. "I want this to work because it feels so real for once in my life. I guess I just feel if I just walk away, I don't have to worry about getting hurt."

Wiping the tears from her face, Chad kissed her forehead and reassured her again that she just had to follow her heart, and then everything else would fall into place.

"Thanks, Chad, for believing in us," Katie said, hugging him tight. "I know there is something there. I can feel it."

"Truce. Now, we need to find some of your flaws.

"Wait, I found one. Never mind," Katie said, smiling. Knowing she had issues of her own, Katie was thinking of ways to find something that wasn't perfect in Chad as well. Teasing him, she started looking for things to make herself feel better.

"What?" he said.

"Persistent," she said.

"No, that's called confident," Chad said, leaning over to kiss her.

"Oh no. We just met a few days ago," Katie said, walking back in her house.

"Brandon, I guess I'll be staying until Sunday," Katie said, watching Chad come in behind her.

"Good. So my good deed is done for the day," Brandon said, confusing Chad.

"What good deed?" Chad said.

"Oh, saving you. Pay me back some other time," Brandon said, leaving.

"Hey, Katie. I know you think I'm persistent, but do you want to fly to California to my house for a couple of days? Then my pilot can fly you home or back here," Chad said, wanting her to see his place. "We can go see Devon while we are there too, even though she just left. It's only Tuesday. You can stay until Thursday or Friday; it's up to you."

"Sure. That would be fun," Katie said. Having strong feelings for Chad, Katie wanted to start out as friends before anything serious would happen. Always having trust issues with men, she wanted to take it slow. "I need to clean here first before I leave, then I'll just go to

Missouri from your house; I have some work to do before my models come back on Monday."

"Well, okay then. I'm going home to pack. Will two hours be good for you?" he asked.

"Sure. I'll make some calls. Are you going to pick me up, or do you want Brandon to bring me over?" Katie said, not knowing where his jet was.

"Well, I live three houses down. If you want, I can pick you up," Chad said, trying not to sound sarcastic.

"Okay then. I'll see you in two hours," Katie said, excited about going to see where he lived.

"Sounds good to me. We will have fun," Chad said, shutting her front door.

Feeling her head spin, Katie quickly sat on the couch. She saw an image of a young boy that was abducted from a road near his house and was never found again. Taken when Katie was young, the image of the boy would forever be in her mind. The mystery of what really happened to him would haunt her and the nation forever. Only nine years old, the boy with brown hair and brown eyes would disappear from his road, only leaving a bike behind. Hearing the house phone ring, Katie quickly snapped back out of her episode.

"Hello? Is Brandon there?" the woman asked, shocked to hear another woman's voice.

"No, but he has his cell phone on him," Katie said, still not back to normal.

"Well, are you his girlfriend?" the woman asked, sounding upset.

"No, he's my son's friend," Katie said, shocked Brandon didn't tell her about a special someone.

"Oh, I'm sorry. You're Katie, right?" she said.

"Yes," Katie said, now really confused.

"Brandon said you were coming up for the week. I'm his girlfriend, Angie," the girl said, not sounding jealous anymore.

"Okay, Angie. I can tell him you called. He just left a few minutes ago," Katie said.

"Oh, that's all right. I'll try his cell phone. Nice talking to you. Brandon said great things about you," Angie said.

"Thanks. Nice talking to you too," Katie said, then she went to put cold water on her face.

Being nosy, Katie decided to call Brandon and ask why she didn't meet Angie.

"Hey, Brandon," Katie said.

"Yes, Katie? Are you okay?" Brandon said.

"Yes. A woman named Angie just called for you. Why haven't you brought her over?" Katie said, trying not to sound rude.

"We just started dating a couple months ago, and this week is about you, not me," Brandon said.

"Okay. I was just curious, and I'm happy for you. She sounds really nice," Katie said.

"She is. I'm sorry I haven't brought her over yet," he said.

"I'm leaving to go to California with Chad, so you can come back home," Katie said.

"One minute you don't like him; the next, you're leaving to his house. Brandon said, laughing.

"Okay. I deserve that," Katie said. "You were right, and thanks for making me realize it before I missed out on Chad; he really likes me for who I am, despite the few minor flaws."

"Everyone has minor flaws, if you want to call them that, Katie. Nobody is perfect," Brandon said. "Everyone has a past that they don't ever tell anyone about. I'm sure Chad's life isn't as perfect as he tells you it is. If it were, he wouldn't be lonely."

"Okay. You should call Angie and bring her over before I leave because I don't know when I'll be back; I'm flying back to Missouri on Friday," Katie said, hoping she would get to meet the mystery woman.

"Okay. Deal. Let me pack up my things here and have her meet me there," Brandon said.

"Okay, and I will call Mark so he doesn't show up here on Sunday when I will already be home," Katie said.

"We will be there within the hour," Brandon said.

"Sounds good. Thanks again for everything," Katie said.

"You say 'thanks' a lot, Katie, which is nice, but without you, where would I be?" he said, saying good-bye.

Calling Mark right away before she forgot, Katie left a voice mail, knowing he was in London with his family.

Packed and ready to go, Katie just walked around and looked at pictures. Checking her messages, she realized Kelsey, her agent, had called.

"Miss Katie, good news! Call me back, please!" she said, sounding excited.

Dialing her number back, Katie was hoping she was going to Italy.

CHAPTER 5

"Hello, Kelsey," Katie said, trying not to get her hopes up.

"Yes, Katie. Good news. They picked your pictures! You're going to Italy!" Kelsey said, just as happy as Katie.

"Are you serious? Oh my gosh; that's so exciting!" Katie said, trying not to scream in Kelsey's ear.

"We leave next month, and we will be gone for two weeks, so make sure your businesses are taken care of, okay?" Kelsey said, excited for her.

"Thanks, and yes, I will work on that," Katie said, grateful for Kelsey. A tall, skinny black woman would be just as determined as Katie about the things they loved in life. A single mother herself, Kelsey would relate to Katie on many levels.

"I'll be in touch, and everything is paid for," Kelsey said, telling her good-bye for now.

Not knowing whom to call first, Katie called Chad. "Guess what?" Katie said, hearing his deep voice.

"What? Do you miss me already? I just left a little while ago," Chad said.

"Yes, but I'll tell you on the way to your house. Brandon has a girlfriend. Did you know that?" Katie said.

"No, I haven't seen a woman there, but good for him!" Chad said, still curious about what she was so excited about. "See you in an hour. Take care."

Calling her kids and family, everyone wasn't as surprised as she was that she made it.

"Katie, congratulations! That says they see the same potential we see," Rachel said.

"Thanks. That means a lot, but I'm going to be gone for two weeks, so I need Casey to run the studio and you to run the library. If you want to hire someone for the time Casey is gone, please do. I don't want to overload anyone else," Katie said, knowing the details could wait.

"We will get it all figured out. No worries, right?" Rachel said.

"Yes, you're right. Thank goodness. I have a month to get ready," Katie said, telling her about leaving to Chad's and then coming home early.

"That sounds like fun. Good for you; it's about time a man came along and swept you off your feet," her sister said.

"Thanks. It's going to take some time to get used to, that's for sure," Katie said. "Please spread the good news to everyone else about Italy. I love you guys!"

Calling her grandma Dee, Katie knew she was her rock, most of her life. Different than her sisters, Katie and her grandma talked about everything from her kids

IN A STRANGER'S EYES

to dating. Almost one hundred years old, Katie's grandma was still getting around well enough to stay at her house with Glen and Hannah.

"Grandma, guess what?" Katie said, always happy to hear her voice.

"What?" she said.

"They picked my pictures! I'm going with Kelsey, my modeling agent, to Italy next month. Can you believe that?" Katie said, trying to contain herself.

"Yes, dear. I can believe that," her grandma said, knowing all the struggles she had to deal with raising her three kids alone so many years. "Congrats to you, sweetie; you deserve it. And who was the good-looking young man at the beach house?"

"Chad. He's really nice," Katie said, still confused on the whole Chad thing.

"Don't think about it too much; just go with the flow, Katie, and you will be fine," her grandma said.

"Thanks, Grandma. You are always so helpful. I'll be back home sometime this weekend. I love you!" Katie said, hearing Brandon and Angie pull up in the driveway. "I have to go for now. I'll come see you when I get home."

With Brandon standing five feet eight inches and Angie being petite like Katie, she was thrilled to see Brandon happy with another female after the sudden loss of his wife several years prior. A woman with short blonde hair, blue eyes, and a great personality, they seemed to make a great couple.

"Katie, Angie. Angie, Katie," Brandon said, smiling as usual.

"Nice to meet you," Katie said.

"Same here," Angie said, hearing Chad pull up in his truck.

"Hey, Brandon. Isn't that the guy from a few houses down?" Angie said, curious as to why he was at Brandon's house.

"Yes, that's who Katie is kind of dating," Brandon said, hugging Katie from behind her.

"Thanks. You know I am going to miss you." Katie turned him around to give him a real hug. "You're like my second son, and you have helped me through so much. Take care of him, okay?" Katie said to Angie.

"Don't worry. We take care of each other," Angie said, thanking Katie for all she did for Brandon.

"No problem. See you later, guys!" Katie said, meeting Chad at his truck.

"Have fun, Katie!" Brandon said, kissing Angie on the cheek.

"Talk to you soon," Katie said, putting her bags in the back of Chad's truck.

"Ready, beautiful?" Chad said, opening her door.

"I'm not used to being spoiled," Katie said, taking her grandma Dee's advice. *I can do this!* Katie kept reminding herself.

"Ready for our trip?" Chad asked.

"Yes, I really think we will have a lot of fun. I've never been to California yet," she said, already excited.

"Doesn't Devon live there?" Chad said.

"Yes, but I don't get out much. I have two businesses that are run out of my house," she said. "I'm excited. Thanks for not giving up on me."

"Katie, we are really in the same boat here. I've only dated a couple of times, just like you, so please excuse me if I mess up for the first…say…month," Chad said, smiling, showing his cute dimples.

"Deal. Me too, but they have to be little mess-ups. I don't deal with drama well!" Katie said, feeling better.

"Me neither. I'm a loner, but I have a few select friends and a lot of hobbies. That's why I love the beach house so much," Chad said, pulling up to his private jet.

"Chad, this is a very nice jet," Katie said. "How long have you had it?"

"About five years," Chad said. "I was blessed with so much like you Katie, but in some different ways."

"Yes, I can see that, but one thing we have in common is that we appreciate it all," Katie said, explaining their differences from her point of view. "I went from having a lot of material things as a child, to having pretty much nothing as I got into my late teens, then I made my own fortune working very hard for several years with the help of my family, of course. I can't and won't take all the credit!"

"That's what makes us appreciate things in life," Chad said, not wanting to sound like he was greedy. "I agree. I donate a lot of money to single parents that are truly trying to get on their feet, not the ones that live off of welfare when they can get up every day and work to better themselves."

"Really?" I donate to that cause too in Missouri that is, amongst several others," Katie said, happy they both were generous people. "It's a great feeling to share my wealth with others."

"Wait, don't you have one too?" he said, laughing at her.

"Yes, but mine is mainly used for my models. This trip was my first flight on my jet in the year I've had it. I'm a busy person," she said, smiling.

"You are an amazing woman, Katie. I'm glad you decided to spend part of your vacation with me. We both deserve each other," Chad said, giving his pilot their luggage.

"You are right," Katie said, grabbing her purse. "Let's do this!"

"Time to board, boss," his pilot said.

"Oh, Katie, this is Cody, my pilot," Chad said, almost forgetting his manners.

"Nice to meet you, ma'am," he said politely.

"Thanks. It's nice to meet you too," Katie said, putting her sunglasses on top of her head.

"Three hour flight, Chad. It should go fast; the weather is nice today," Cody said.

Finding their seats in Chad's jet, Katie was finally able to relax a little more.

"Are you ready to see another new place?" Chad asked her, excited she was going with him to see his house.

"Yes," Katie said, smiling ear to ear. "I'm shocking myself in several ways this week, actually. It's a great feeling!"

"So, you had some good news you wanted to tell me earlier?" Chad asked, curious as to the new direction her life would be taking her again.

"Yes, I came to Florida a day early to meet my agent from many years ago for a photo shoot, and to make a long story short, I was picked to go to Italy to represent a story on women that have been models for over twenty years!" she said.

"Wow, Katie," he said, happy for Katie. "That is fantastic, although I can see why they picked you, a woman that is strong willed, outgoing, and beautiful to boot!"

"Thanks, Chad. God has been so good to me. I sometimes wonder I was so blessed with the things I have been able to achieve."

Falling asleep the first part of the movie, Katie was surprised to wake up already at his house.

"We are here," Chad said, shaking her.

"Oh sorry. I guess I was more tired than I thought," Katie said, adjusting her eyes.

"Ready for a tour?" Chad asked, helping her out of his jet.

"Chad, this is truly amazing!" Katie said, putting her sunglasses on to enjoy all the beauty his land had.

Looking around, Katie saw some of Chad's friends golfing on his personal golf course. Waving at Chad and Katie, they both waved back.

"I have several lakes," Chad said as he loaded up his Cadillac with their luggage. "My golf course and my house. It's a lot of land for one person, but I love it!"

"Thanks. I can say the same thing for you," Chad said, smiling at her. "I have eight hundred acres, a golf course, riding trails, and lakes for fishing or boating."

"This is great. You should be proud," Katie said, taking out her camera.

"A lady with a camera. Chad, you met your match," Cody said, knowing they had great chemistry. Chad loaded up the Cadillac with all their luggage.

"I am very proud. Thanks. But you have the same things," Chad said.

"Yes, some of the same things. I think it's different for me because I don't get out to enjoy mine as much as I should," Katie said, snapping pictures like a celebrity was at his house.

"Well, you should. All your talent shouldn't be stuck inside all of the time," he said, still not knowing what to say without offending her.

Driving around for nearly thirty minutes, Katie looked in awe as he pointed at some of his gardens out in a field.

"I spend most of my time when I'm not working doing many things I love such as golfing, fishing, writing, reading, and several other hobbies," he said, showing her around as she was reminded of her own land. "My photography is my first passion though."

"This reminds me a lot of my own place," Katie said, finally feeling that was okay to feel her emotions toward Chad. "We have more in common than I thought we had!"

"See if you just trust, everything else will fall into place," Chad said, chuckling. "It's a proven fact, you know?"

"Yes, I know that is a fact," Katie said, feeling as if she's known this stranger for years. "You are so right. Thanks for not giving up on me. That means a lot to me."

"I'm just speechless!" Katie said.

"Don't be, really. It's just a house; nothing spectacular," Chad said.

"Whatever. Are you sure there is not a girlfriend hiding in this big house?" Katie said.

"Yes, I'm sure," he said.

Katie's week flew by as her and Chad bonded more than before in Florida. Enjoying their time together, she let her fear of getting hurt go and decided to start the trust process once more. Learning how to golf, Katie felt a new direction was taking her away from the life she once had. Having fun on her vacation, Chad took her on several rides on his Harley throughout California. Smiling what seemed like the whole time there, Katie felt like a new woman that she has never met before. Getting to know the new side of her, Katie didn't realize how truly lonely she was at her house.

"I have to go home tomorrow. It's Friday already," Katie said, depressed. Walking from his spare bedroom where she stayed while at Chad's house, Katie got packed and ready to go home. Going to the kitchen, Katie informed him that her trip had to end the next day, so she could get a couple days ahead on her work at home before her vacation was over.

"I know, and you were going to leave yesterday, but I'm glad you decided to stay," Chad said, starting dinner. "Do you like salads?"

"Yes. You can cook too? You never cease to amaze me," she said, smiling.

"It's salad, not steak. That's later," Chad said, already dreading her departure.

"Ha-ha, yes. Your sense of humor is addicting too," Katie said, leaning over to kiss him on the cheek.

"Okay. Now you have to move in," Chad said, laughing.

"I can't do that. I have my life in the country, remember?" Katie said.

"Aw, yes. But tomorrow, I get a tour of your house, right?" Chad said, hoping she wouldn't mind him coming along.

"Sure, if you're ready to see the Midwest," Katie said, still smiling.

"Actually, I've been many places, but not to Missouri yet. It should be fun," Chad said, making their food.

"How's this going to work?" Katie said, doubting herself again.

"Remember, we both have jets, silly," he said, trying to stay confident for both of them.

"Yes, no worries. Right. I forgot," Katie said, trying not to get anxious again. "That's a great idea, you coming over. You can see how us county folk live."

"So, do you cook at home, or do you have a chef?" he asked curiously.

"Well, yes, I have a chef for my models, but I do cook for myself," Katie said, always independent.

"You are so talented and determined. Have you always been like that?" he asked.

"Yes, pretty much my whole life," Katie said, proud of all her accomplishments.

"That explains why your kids are the same way," he said, amazed at how respectful they all were. "Still daylight. Want to go for a jog after dinner?"

"Hey, can you take off work a couple of days and stay at my house? You have already met my family," she said, hoping he could.

"Well, I am self-employed. Sure, I can do that. Thanks for the invite," Chad said, excited he was going to get to spend more time with her.

"Oh, I need to go check my phone messages," Katie said, not having her phone on her all day.

Walking upstairs to the room, Katie closed the door behind her for privacy. Feeling as if her head would explode, Katie saw a woman's face pleading for the safe return of her kids, knowing she drove them off in a lake in her car, saying a man hijacked her kids and made her get out of her own car.

"Please stop! Not here, not now!" Katie said as she fell to the ground grasping for air. Trying to keep herself pulled together, Katie crawled up to her knees—only to fall once more.

"Katie, dinner is ready!" Chad said, worried about her taking so long.

Opening his door, he saw Katie shaking as if she were having a seizure.

"Katie, come back to me," is all he could say, scared she was dying. With her eyes rolling back in her head, Chad called an ambulance, not knowing what else to do. "Katie, you're scaring me! Please, please wake up!" Chad said, not aware if this was normal for her episodes. Talking on the phone with a dispatcher, Chad did exactly what they told him to do. Coming out of her spell, Katie blinked her eyes and stopped shaking.

"I think she is coming out if it. This happens sometimes, her family said," Chad said, getting up to get her some water. With the medics already downstairs, Chad let them in to check her out, just to be on the safe side.

"Sir, do you know her medical background?" the medic asked as Chad tried to remember all of her kids' names. Finding Devon in her phone, Chad called, hoping she could help solve the mystery.

"Hello, Devon. This is Chad, and your mom is at my house. She had an episode here, and I called the ambulance. She's better now, but there is a medic that has some questions about your mom's health," Chad said, handing the phone to the medic. Asking her lots of questions, the medic saw Katie trying to get up off the floor.

"Ma'am, do you know your name?" the strange man asked her.

"Yes, my name is Katie," she said, looking around the room.

"That's good. We are paramedics. We're here to check your vitals to make sure your going to be all right, okay?

So just try to relax," the nice man said, checking her blood pressure and oxygen level.

"I'm okay now, really," Katie said, trying to stand up.

"This will only take a few minutes, and we will be leaving," he said, hoping she would cooperate.

"Okay, sorry," Katie said as they took everything off.

"Everything looks good, but you should see a doctor soon," he said.

"Chad, I'm all right. I'm sorry to scare you. It just happens so fast that I can't stop it," Katie said, taking her phone from the medic.

"Thanks. Who's on the phone?" she asked, confused.

"Devon, your daughter. I had to call someone that knew your medical background. You looked like you were having a seizure, so I called nine-one-one," he said, trying to make sense of everything.

Walking the medics back out of his house, Katie talked to Devon, reassuring her she was all right.

"Katie, I didn't know what else to do but call nine-one-one. I panicked," he said, still shaking.

"I'm sorry, Chad. I don't know what else to say," Katie said, hugging him.

"I'm glad you're back. I missed you," he said, relieved she was standing there.

"Aw, thanks. It will take me a few minutes to get up and moving around, but I'll be back to myself in no time," Katie said, trying to convince herself she was going to be all right.

"Dinner is ready, if you want to eat. When you get your strength back, that is," Chad said, trying not to get on her nerves.

Getting up, Katie splashed cold water on her face. "I'm going to freshen up. I'll meet you in the kitchen, okay?" Katie said.

"Okay. I'll see you in a little bit," Chad said, closing the bedroom door softly.

After watching his wife fight cancer for so many years, he was starting to wonder if he could handle Katie's issues. Confused, he sat down at the kitchen table, patiently waiting for her return.

Hearing her footsteps, Chad saw her back to normal. "Hey. You look much better," is all Chad could say.

"Thanks. I feel a lot better," Katie said, hoping he could deal with everything.

"I'm here for you, and I'm not going to think of you any different, okay?" Chad said, knowing he wasn't back to his playful self yet.

"Thanks. That means so much to me. You have no idea," she said, relieved already.

"I warmed up dinner, if you're hungry," Chad said.

"Thanks, and yes, I'm starving!" Katie said, touching his broad shoulders behind his chair.

"Tell me if I'm crossing the line here, but have you seen a doctor for these episodes?" Chad said, trying not to make her upset.

"No, you're not crossing the line, and yes, I have seen several doctors. In fact, they all seem to think it's temporary," Katie said, trying to make sense of it herself. "It's been a year, and I think they get worse, then I can go two weeks with none."

"Thanks for the explanation, and I'm so glad you are sitting here," Chad said, pushing his plate aside.

The rest of the evening went fast. Katie headed upstairs for bed.

"Good night, Chad," she said, going there separate ways to their own rooms.

"Good night, sweetie. Sleep well," he said. "Tomorrow, we are leaving for the country. I'm excited."

"Good, I think you will like it. Sleep well," Katie said, not closing the door all the way.

Grabbing her cell phone, Katie saw she had several missed calls from her kids and family, who were worried about the call Devon received. Calling them all back one by one, they were at ease. She was going to be fine. Telling them all good night, Katie rolled over and fell fast asleep.

Not waking up once throughout the night, Katie awoke in the morning to the birds singing outside. *Wow, I can't believe I got nine hours of straight sleep,* Katie thought to herself as she got up to pack for her trip back home.

Walking downstairs, Katie saw Chad was gone. "Chad?" Katie said, wondering where he could have went.

"I'm in here, beautiful, making us some coffee," he said, coming around the corner.

"Already packed."

"Me too," he said, kissing her on the cheek.

"Yes, and coffee sounds good about now," Katie said. "I like it here."

"Good because I like it here too," Chad said, smiling. "So are you ready to go home?"

"Yes, my vacation has been wonderful, but it's time for me to go back to reality," Katie said, excited. "I'm glad you are going to come see how I live for a couple of days."

"Me too. Change is usually a good thing, so they say," Chad said, getting his phone out to call Cody. "We will be ready in thirty minutes if you can fly us to Missouri."

"Sure thing. I'll see you there, then" Cody said, happy for Chad.

Cleaning up the house, Chad and Katie headed outside. "Another pretty day. How do we get so lucky?" Katie said, smiling.

"It's not luck, honey; it's California. You're used to Missouri weather, where one day it's raining and the next it's snowing," Chad said, chuckling.

"You're right. Our weather is unpredictable at times, to say the least," Katie said, laughing with him.

Getting back on his jet, Katie felt a little nervous still.

"No worries. By the time we fly back and forth a few times, you will be a pro at this," Chad said, curious as to what her house would be like.

"You're right, as usual," Katie said, knowing she worried herself over the craziest things sometimes.

"You're learning early. I like that," Chad said sarcastically.

"Whatever. I am right sometimes too; we have to share that responsibility," Katie said jokingly.

"Deal," Chad said, shaking her hand.

Staying awake the whole flight, Katie saw her airport.

"We are here, Miss Katie," Cody said.

"Great! That went fast!" Katie said, gathering her magazines and purse.

Amazed at the countryside, Chad couldn't believe all of her land. "This is amazing!" he said, watching a man pull up to pick them up. Seeing Mark pull up in her white Ford F150, Chad grabbed their things and walked over to meet Mark, Katie's pilot.

"Nice to meet you Mark," he said, being polite as always. "Thanks for the ride. My name is Chad."

"You're welcome," Mark said, shocked Katie brought a man of interest to her house. "It's nice to meet you too, Chad."

"Katie, your land is truly amazing!" he said.

"Hey, Mark. Thanks for the ride," Katie said.

"Anytime, boss," Mark said, smiling.

"Mark, I want you to meet Chad and Cody," Katie said.

After shaking hands, they all loaded up as Cody was preparing to head home.

"How was your family vacation to London?" Katie asked curiously.

"It was great. We brought you back something," Mark said.

Unloading their bags, Katie and Chad headed in her backdoor. "Thanks for the ride. I'll call you later," Katie said, waving good-bye.

"Are you ready for your tour?" Katie asked Chad, smiling.

"Yes, actually, I am," Chad said, following behind her.

"Here's your room. It's Ashley's room when she used to stay here before she got a townhouse three miles away from here," Katie said. "I would give you Jacob's room, but it's on the lower level, hidden really well."

"Really? I bet he liked that," Chad said, amazed at how her house was set up. "Did you design this yourself?"

"Actually, I did. It's been finished for a year, but it took nine months to build," Katie said, proud of all her hard work. "This is the library where Rachel and Casey do the customer service orders."

"I have published three children's books and one novel, but I recently started the sequel to my novel. I also have a book factory that my mom, Jackie, runs an hour north of here," Katie said, trying to explain how her book business worked.

"Katie, this is truly amazing. Your whole set up here, and you designed your house for all of these reasons?" he asked curiously.

"Yes, this house has been dreamed up since I was young," Katie went on to say as she took him downstairs to show him the rest of her house. "It hasn't been easy to get this far, but a lot of my money goes to several charities such as struggling authors, models that can't afford to get their foot in the door. I share my wealth for sure. I love to be simple; that's the way I have always been. It's taking me quite a while to get used to actually living my dream, but I keep on working to better everything I have going."

"Impressive!" Chad said, loving the design she made.

"Thanks. All that's up here is my room, Devon and Ashley's room, and the library. I left this open for the bay window, so it's not so cramped," she went on to say while giving him a tour of her house.

Walking down the spiral staircase to the main floor, Katie showed him her office hidden behind the front door.

"This is the living room. I made the main floor hardwood and the two steps to the carpeted area for the couches and entertainment center, along with my pictures, of course," she said, feeling like a real estate lady trying to sell a house.

"And this what you saw coming in the backdoor. This is my kitchen, laundry room, and food pantry," Katie went on to say.

Turning on the light to go down her spiral staircase to the studio, Katie was so proud to show off her love of art. "I have several rooms down here. I have this first room where my pictures are actually taken."

Turning on the light to the pool area, Chad's eyes lit up. "This is where the models finish their photo shoots because their hair gets wet, and then it would be pointless to start over," she said, moving right along with the tour.

"This room, next to the pool area, where I keep hair, makeup, and wardrobe to fit all shapes and sizes for both male and female models. I do this first, two models at a time, usually the ones I can pair together or alone. Depends on the shots they want. Next is the darkroom, where I'm sure you know what I do in there. That's my last step of the long process."

"Can I stop you?" Chad said, shocked. "So you do this all yourself: their hair, makeup, wardrobe, pictures, and proofs, all in one day?"

"Yes. I charge them all a flat rate, and they all have to have at least two years experience so I don't have to coach them all day long," Katie said.

Turning on the light where the models stayed while waiting their turn to do their photo shoot, Katie was proud of her room full of video games and the huge window that they could only see out, as to not disturb the other models while they were doing their shoot.

"The reason for that is when I get some models under eighteen, I have the parents watch from there so it doesn't distract me or their kids," Katie said, almost done with her house tour.

Walking down a few more stairs, Katie turned on a light that showed a full living area including a kitchen, living room, bathroom and bedroom designed by her son. "This is Jacob's room when he comes in town off tour, which is only a few times a year."

"Wow, Jacob is very creative, just like the rest of his family," Chad said, still amazed at her house.

"Yes, he's been a model since he was a teenager. Then before he went on tour, he was a personal trainer for the local fitness club."

Looking at Jacob's trophy case, Chad was amazed at all his baseball, soccer, and weightlifting trophies.

"Are Ashley and Devon's room like Jacob's?" Chad asked, still in awe of Jacob's many talents hidden below a spectacular house.

"No, the girls' trophies are on my entertainment center in the living room. The girls' room is pretty plain; they share the same bathroom between both of their rooms. Devon, I don't think she has stayed in the room made for her yet; she's been in California since I moved in. Ashley, who lives pretty close, has stayed in her room a few times," Katie went on to say. "Well, that completes the tour of my house, on the inside anyway."

Walking upstairs to the main floor, Katie walked out the backdoor to show Chad the pool and some of the view with her trees and jumps for her ATVs. Walking around to the front of her house, Katie showed Chad the circle driveway and the design of her house. Opening her garage, Katie only had her BMW and Mustang stored neatly whenever she wanted to go to town. Looking at the landscaping, Chad was amazed at the flowers so neatly tended to.

"We are almost done with my house," she said.

Walking him over to the six-car garage, Katie opened it and showed off her classic cars collecting dust. "There's the Camaro, Mustang Nova, and Chevelle, and at the far end is Jacob's Viper; he bought it himself for when he's home, which isn't nearly enough," Katie said, smiling. "I keep the ATVs, dirt bikes, and dune buggies in here for whenever my nephew and his kids come over, or if my sister's teenage kids want to ride, I get mine out. Other than that, they all stay locked away. Ready for a tour of my land, city boy?"

"Yes, let's do this!" he said excitedly.

Riding through the woods, Katie showed him everyone's houses that were also equipped with in-ground pools and three-story houses. Stopping by her mom's house first, Chad and Katie knocked and walked in.

"Mom, Sam, are you home?" Katie said. She was startled by Sam.

"Hey, Katie. How was your vacation?" he asked. "Your mom is upstairs." Sam introduced himself to Chad.

"I'll be right back!" Katie said, running upstairs to see her mom.

Her mom was lying down, and Katie wasn't sure if she was awake or asleep. "Mom, are you awake?" Katie said, watching her mom sound asleep in her bed. Not wanting to wake her up, Katie went back downstairs.

"So, how was the Bahamas?" she asked him, giving him a hug.

"It was beautiful. Your mom is worn out," Sam said.

"Okay, we are going to see Grandma Dee and the gang," Katie said, knowing she missed everybody. "Love you. I'll call Mom in the morning before she heads back to work on Monday," Katie said, hopping back on the ATV. Passing by Casey and Rachel's houses, Katie showed Chad the lake made for all her family that loved to fish. Pulling up to the circle driveway, Katie rang the doorbell. Her dad, Glen opened the door, happy to see her, as usual. Giving Katie a hug and greeting Chad, her stepmom, Hannah, and her Grandma Dee set a couple of extra places at their table as they filled it with biscuits and gravy, sausage, bacon, and eggs. With Katie saying grace, they all sat at their seats grateful to have each other's company. Visiting for nearly an hour, Katie and Chad helped clean up the meal before they left their house.

"Well, we have to head back to my house. It's been a long day," Katie said ready to go home and relax.

Looking at the time on her cell phone, Katie couldn't believe it was seven o'clock in the evening.

"It's been a great day. Now I need a shower after all the riding," Katie said. "Do you want to hang out tonight and watch a movie? Tomorrow is only Sunday."

"Sure, a movie sounds great," Chad said, happy she enjoyed his company as much as she did his.

"Yes, that is very true," Katie said, smiling ear to ear. "We think a lot alike!"

"You have a really nice place, Katie," Chad said, helping her put the ATV back in the garage.

"Thanks. I love it here. So peaceful," she said, ready for a shower and movie. "So I'm going to take a shower, and I'll meet you in the living room in thirty minutes, all right?" Katie said, winking at him.

"Sounds good to me," he said.

Checking her voice mails, Katie noticed she had several missed calls from all her kids, Brandon, and her mother. Deciding to call them back the next day, Katie hurried to meet Chad downstairs after her long shower. Walking to the top of the staircase, Katie saw Chad sound asleep on the couch. Tired herself, Katie went to her room and went right to sleep in her own bed.

Only up a few times during the night, Katie slept in as long as she could, knowing the following day would be back to running around. Enjoying the country one more day, Katie and Chad got to know each other better.

"Where did the day go?" Chad said, knowing she had to get plenty of rest for her busy day at work.

Eating dinner together, Katie and Chad cleaned up the dishes together. Katie reached over to give Chad a hug. Looking into his eyes, they began to feel the sparks as they kissed for the first time. With Katie fighting the chemistry so long, she finally realized he wasn't going anywhere and that he now gained her trust enough to know everything was going to be all right.

"Good night, Chad," Katie said, walking away from him to get ready for bed. "Good night, beautiful," Chad said, still shocked they finally took a big step in

their relationship.

Getting in her shower, Katie lay in her king-size bed, thinking about Chad, and fell asleep.

Katie woke up to her alarm clock. She made her herself get up for her daily morning jog. Walking by Ashley's room on the way downstairs, Katie saw Chad sleeping so peacefully. Smiling, she went to start her stretches. Grabbing her water bottle, Katie went on her four-mile jog.

Coming back in, Katie headed to her room to take a shower and get ready for everyone to arrive. Hearing Casey, Rachel, and Sheri talking, Katie knew her normal routine needed to kick in. Throwing herself together, Katie headed to the kitchen for her morning meeting before her models arrived.

"So, how was everyone's vacation?" Katie asked, smiling.

Agreeing they all had a great week off, Katie headed to the studio to get ready.

"Katie, don't you think you should wake Chad up so he doesn't feel so out of place with everyone here?" Rachel said.

"Yes, let's go, ladies!" Katie said, knowing he would be shocked to see all of them.

"Chad, wake up!" she said, trying not to scare him.

"Hey. Good morning, beautiful," he said. seeing her two sister's behind her.

"Good morning to you too. We have work this morning, remember?" Katie said. "Do you want help in the studio today? Or I can call my nephew, and you guys can hang out; my day usually ends by five."

"Sure. Let me get ready, and I will help you today. I'll meet you in your studio in thirty minutes, okay?" he said, still waking up. Not used to so many people, Chad loved to hear all the laughing in her house. With Rachel and Casey like her best friends, they talked about everything.

"Katie, we are heading up to work. Have fun with Chad today," Rachel said teasing her.

"Thanks, ladies. See you at lunch. You should really be more sociable and eat Sheri's food; it's really good!" Katie said, smiling. "Have a great day at work."

CHAPTER 6

Smiling all the way down the spiral staircase to the main floor, Katie heard Sheri starting her meals for the day.

"Good morning. How was your vacation?" she asked, curious as to why she was so happy.

Usually indifferent most mornings, Katie seemed a lot different. "It was great, how about you?" Katie said, waiting for Chad to come down.

"Great. I took my kids to Disneyland with my bonus. It was great. Thank you so much!" Sheri said, giving her a hug.

"Oh, you're welcome. You are a big part of our team," Katie said.

"Katie!" they both heard coming down to the living room.

"Hey, Chad. I'm in the kitchen with my chef," Katie said, still happy.

"Good morning, ladies," Chad said, keeping his eyes on Katie.

"Good morning Chad," Katie said. "This is Sheri. She's my chef. She makes up my models meals every day."

"Hi, Sheri," Chad said, happy to meet her. "Nice to meet you."

"Nice. Did you pick him up in Florida?" she said, winking at her.

"Yes, actually, she did. At her beach house," he said, teasing Katie.

"Okay, it was mutual really. We are heading to the studio. Mark will be here shortly," Katie said, turning on some classic rock to start her morning. "Are you sure you don't mind hanging out? I will enjoy your company."

"Are you kidding? I get to watch you hard at work all day. I'm the lucky one," he said, winking at her. "If you need help, just ask. I don't want to get in your way; I think you can handle this."

"Are you ready? I stay busy, so please feel free to visit Sheri, Rachel, and Casey. None of us are used to a good-looking man walking around, making our day," Katie said, trying to put on her professional face.

"Oh, you have a serious side," Chad said, laughing. "I like that side too. Are there any more personalities I should be worried about?"

"Nah, you have met them all. I think you're safe," she said, knowing he has seen her in her darkest moments.

Meeting her models at the staircase, Katie started with her normal tour, so everyone stayed on schedule all day. "Ladies and gentlemen, this is my friend, Chad. He's a photographer as well, but he's just watching me work for a couple of days, so please get yourself comfortable," she said, hoping she could concentrate with him sitting on a chair all day, watching her multitask. "Chad, will you help me set up a few heavy chairs? I want to try something new."

"Sure," Chad said, happy to be there.

"Lunchtime," Sheri said from the top of the stairs.

"Okay, let's take a break!" Katie told them as they went to see what Sheri prepared for them. "What is it today?"

"Italian today," Sheri said.

"Great. Everyone help themselves," Katie said, directing them to the plates and silverware. The models couldn't have had more fun.

"You have a beautiful house, Ms. Roth," a young female model said.

"Thanks. It takes several people to keep it running. You only see a few of us," Katie said, rarely talking on a personal level with her clients.

Looking out the backdoor, Chad stood there and shook his head at the countryside. "I still can't believe I've missed out on this my whole life. Missouri is a beautiful state," he said, walking outside by her in-ground pool. "Hey, Katie. Do you mind if I take one of your ATVs for a ride?"

"Sure. Grab a fishing pole, if you want to. I had my lakes stocked with big catfish because Jacob is a huge fisherman," she said, heading back in to start the second part of her day.

"Thanks. I love your place. I thought mine was nice!" he said.

"Yours is nice too. We both have the same taste," Katie said, winking at him. "Okay, five more minutes, and we will work with the last three models."

"This is amazing. Who would have thought a woman could do all of this?" a male model said, shocking all of the women at the table.

Sheri, knowing Katie was very independent, hoped she would keep her good reputation and not say something she would regret.

"Yes, men and women are equal in every way possible," Katie said, holding her head up high. "Let's do this, gang!"

"Katie, good answer. I'm proud of you," Sheri said, knowing Katie never discriminated against anyone, no matter the case. Turning on the music, Katie did the last three models' hair, makeup, and wardrobe. With the second part of her day flying by, Katie looked at the time, knowing Mark should be coming soon.

"Okay, everyone. We will go to the darkroom and do your pictures, comp card, and CDs," she said, glad her workday was coming to an end.

"Katie, I just pulled up!" Mark said across her phone.

"Thanks. We will be done in about thirty minutes," she said, wondering where Chad went to fish. Finishing up her pictures, Katie walked the models up to Mark, praising them for all their hard work. Watching them load up in the truck, Katie waved good-bye.

"Nice-looking man you have," Sheri said, cleaning up for the day.

"Thanks. I need to get my riding clothes on and see where he went fishing. I have six lakes out there; I would feel bad if he got lost," Katie said. "He's a keeper, I think."

"Don't think, just enjoy!" Sheri said, always looking up to her.

"I will enjoy. I promise. I've lost on a few good men over the years because I thought the worst instead of the best," Katie said, excited to go riding in the pretty weather.

"You didn't miss out; you just paved your way to Chad. Good job," Sheri said, grabbing her purse to go home to her kids.

"Thanks, Sheri. Have a great day," Katie said, running upstairs to see her sisters before they left for the day.

"Hey. Has it been crazy in here today?" Katie said, seeing them still hard at work.

"Yes, but I think we can stop for the day," Rachel said, turning off her computer.

"Me too. Wow, the first day back is so hard after a great week off work," Casey said, grabbing her purse.

"Where's your man?" Rachel said, teasing Katie.

"He went fishing somewhere. I'm going to see if I can find him," Katie said excitedly.

"Well, have fun. You deserve Chad and Italy," Rachel said, giving her a hug.

"Thanks, ladies. What would I do without you two?" Katie said, so grateful for all her family.

"You would be an even busier person," Casey said, laughing at her.

"Yeah, very true. Have a great evening. See you in the morning," Katie said, going to her room to dig out her riding clothes.

Getting all geared up, Katie stopped to check her phone and called Chad to see where he was at with no answer on his cell phone. Katie headed out on her ATV in hopes she could find him in the daylight. Trying to remember where all her lakes were, Katie enjoyed the beautiful day with still no luck finding Chad. Katie called Rachel and Casey to help. Her nieces and nephews and brother-in-law all aided in the search. Katie began to worry as the sun went down. Katie turned off her ATV in hopes to hear Chad lost in the woods.

"Chad!" she yelled, hoping for a response. With nothing but silence of birds and frogs, Katie wondered if she should be so worried. Calling Ted, trying not to panic, she heard him say, "Katie, he's a grown man. He will come to somebody's house. You already took him on a tour, right?" Ted, her brother-in-law, said.

"Yes. Wait. I hear another ATV," Katie said, hoping it was Chad. Seeing the lights, Katie waited and prayed it was him and that he was all right.

"Katie, is it him?" Ted said on the phone. Pulling up along side her, Katie was relieved it was him. He wondered why she had such a worried look on her face.

"Yes, Ted. Okay, call off the troops," Katie said, feeling as if a big weight was lifted off her shoulders.

"I'm sorry. I didn't mean to worry anyone. I got a little lost out here, but I'm happy to see you, so I can take a shower and cuddle up next to you," Chad said, just as happy to see her.

"I've not been out here at night this far from my house, so let's hope we find our way back to my house," Katie said jokingly.

"Please say you're kidding. I'm tired, hungry, and lonely," Chad said, kissing her before they began their journey.

"Okay. Let's go eat some dinner. I've been out here for four hours," Katie said, glad she didn't have to call more people to her house. Only sharing one kiss before that night, Katie felt as if she could melt. Chad, a man that had just met Katie a week prior, felt as if her life was changing right in front of her eyes.

"I've been out here ten hours, not that I'm complaining. I loved fishing all day," Chad said, turning his ATV back on.

Following her marks, they found their way back to her house. After putting everything away, they went inside to eat leftovers from Sheri's lunch.

"I have to leave tomorrow; I'm booked the rest of this week," Chad said.

"I know. Do you want me to call Mark to have him fly you back, or are you going to call Cody?" Katie said, washing up, ready to relax a few minutes before she headed to take a shower.

"Cody will be here by noon, but thanks; I'm not ready to leave yet," Chad said, sad to go back to his empty house.

"Okay, well, I'm going to get ready for bed soon. I'm glad you're all right and no coyotes got you," Katie said, laughing.

"Ha-ha, that's not funny, really," he said, following behind her.

"I know. They are gross. Have you ever seen one?" Katie asked, only ever seeing one in her whole life.

"No, I have heard they are really scary," Chad said, heading to his room, exhausted.

"Yes, you have no idea!" Katie said, tired after a long night. "They look like a wild, evil dog with hardly any hair. One of the scariest creatures I have ever seen in my life!" Katie remembered driving down a long country road and seeing one cross the street.

Walking into her room, Katie closed the door out of habit. Feeling as if she were drunk, Katie saw a child's face, only around nine years old; a cute girl with blonde hair and blue eyes. She would shoot her parents in their sleep. Trying to figure out how much evil could come from such a beautiful angel, Katie tried to get the image out of her head. Hearing her cell phone ring, Katie, shaking, grabbed it to see who was calling.

"Mom, thank goodness you called," Katie said, happy to hear her voice.

"Is everything all right? You sound like something is terribly wrong," Jackie said.

"No, I'm okay. We lost Chad, whom you haven't met yet; he's leaving around noon tomorrow. If you want to come over before you head up north, that would make my day. I've missed you!" Katie said, not seeing her over a week.

"Sure, honey. I'll see you around seven in the morning. I love you and can't wait to see you. I've missed you too," Jackie said, happy for her.

"Okay, thanks for calling," Katie said, slowly gathering her nightclothes to take a shower.

Taking a cool shower, Katie was happy to get that image out of her head. Katie dried her hair and crawled into bed, knowing five o'clock would come early. She fell fast asleep.

Katie awoke in the middle of the night, as usual. Overly tired, she fell right back to sleep, grateful she had a few more hours to relax.

Dragging the next morning, Katie stopped by Chad's room, watching him sleep like a baby. Skipping her morning jog, Katie made breakfast and went to her room to get ready for another busy day. Stopping by Chad's room again, Katie decided to wake him up so she could spend a little more time with him before he headed back to California.

"Chad, wake up. Are you hungry? Breakfast is done downstairs. I have to get ready for work. My mom is stopping by to see you," Katie said, giving him a good-morning kiss.

"Okay, I'm getting up!" Chad said.

"I'll meet you in the kitchen, okay? My crew will be showing up in an hour, and it takes me about that long to get ready. I want to look respectful to my models; they look up to me, which is a great thing," Katie said, heading to her room to find something nice but comfortable to wear.

"I look up to you, and I'm your boyfriend, or at least I think I am," Chad said, unsure of his own comment.

Don't think; enjoy it, Katie said thinking to herself.

"And yes, you are my boyfriend, if that's all right."

Happy, Chad got dressed for the day and packed his clothes for his trip back home. Walking down the spiral staircase, Chad did what Katie did almost every day: stop and admire the view. Looking down the spiral staircase, Chad loved how her living room was set up filled with her family portraits. Leaving his luggage on the couch, Chad went to the kitchen to see what Katie prepared his for breakfast. Smelling a plate of pancakes, sausage, and toast, his stomach growled. When he heard Katie's footsteps coming down the stairs, he felt a sharp pang in his stomach. He knew he was falling for her way too fast. Chad looked up to see her in jeans, high heels, and a nice shirt. With her hair down and straightened, Chad didn't realize her hair went down to the middle of her back.

"You look nice," Chad said.

"Thanks," Katie said, knowing her mother would be there anytime. Katie saw Chad grinning ear to ear, as her personality began to shine more and more with him around.

Knock! Knock!

"Come in, Mom," Katie said, giving her a hug. Introducing the two, they all chatted until Sheri, Casey, and Rachel arrived. "I need to run down to the studio

IN A STRANGER'S EYES

and turn on my equipment real fast," Katie said as Casey stopped her.

"I'll do it. What I hear is you want me to run the photography business while you're away in Italy," Casey said.

"Thanks, sis!" Katie said, enjoying her company.

Doing their morning meeting, Katie explained some of the changes that would be happening over the next couple of months. Overwhelmed with her studio, Katie decided to have her models only there three times a week instead of five. Sheri, now concerned, asked Katie to put her in training with Rachel, knowing she would need the help while Katie was away for a couple of weeks.

"We will go back to normal when everything calms down," Katie said, confusing her staff. "It's only temporary. No worries. My models are booked Monday through Friday for the next few months. So Casey isn't overwhelmed, she will only have five instead of seven models. In the future, I'm only going to do the studio three days a week."

"Sounds good, Katie," they all said, heading to their stations.

"You have it all figured out, huh?" Chad said, getting up to follow her downstairs.

Beep! Beep! she heard on the phone.

"Hey, Mark," Katie said, knowing he would give her at least thirty minutes notice before they would just show up. "Thanks, Mark. See you soon," Katie said feeling kind of sad that Chad had to leave.

"Hey, Friday after work, do you want to come stay with me for the weekend? It's a nice getaway place," he said, hoping she would say yes.

"Sure, let me check my schedule, but I'm pretty sure it's open," Katie said, smiling.

"Good because I called Cody, and he's on his way. I don't want to fall behind on my work," Chad said. "Before your house gets chaotic, I want to tell you that you are an amazing woman, and I owe you for rescuing me last night."

"Thanks. I'll have Mark fly me there after work Friday, okay?" Katie said, hearing the models come in the backdoor.

"Sounds great. Do you need any help while I'm waiting for my ride?" Chad asked, knowing he would be bored.

"Sure, thanks. I think I'm going to spice things up a bit today. The help will be greatly appreciated," Katie said, welcoming her models and starting her daily tour. "Everyone, this is Chad. He will only be here for a little while this morning; he's a photographer as well, so we are going to have him set up the drops for something different," Katie said, surprising Chad.

Looking at her oddly, Chad moved things around similar to his own studio.

"Very nice, Chad. A man's touch is always nice every once in a while," Katie said, liking his ideas.

"Thanks, Katie. I'm glad you like it," Chad said, hearing his phone going off.

He walked upstairs to talk to Cody, his pilot. Coming back down, Chad told everyone good-bye.

"Let me call Mark and ask him to drive you to the airport. I would hate for you to get lost in the woods again," Katie joked.

"Thank you. Although, the worried look on your face was priceless," Chad said He kissed Katie on the cheek good-bye.

"Everyone take a five minute break, please, I will be back shortly," Katie said as she followed Chad upstairs to meet Mark. Going outside with Chad, Katie gave him a big hug and kiss goodbye.

"I'm going to miss you!" she said, upset he was going back home.

Getting back to her work, Katie was surprised at how fast the day flew by.

Cleaning up after everyone left, Katie went upstairs to talk with Sheri.

"Thanks for giving me more hours while you're away next month. I'm sure Casey appreciates the lighter load too. I'm shocked how well you maintain everything here," Sheri said, grabbing her purse and heading out the backdoor.

Heading upstairs to say bye to her sisters, Katie could see something was wrong with Rachel. "Rachel, what's the matter?" Katie said, watching her wipe the tears from her eyes.

"I'm pregnant!" she said. "I just got the test results from the doctor over the phone."

"Oh my gosh. That's great news!" Katie said, hugging her sister. Does Ted know yet?"

"Yes, I just called him at home. I'm just in shock," Rachel said.

"Is Ted coming to pick you up, or do you want me to drive you home?" Katie asked, not wanting her to drive.

"Casey drove today, and we are getting ready to leave soon, but thanks," Rachel said, crying happy tears of joy.

"I'm going to change for an evening jog, ladies. I love you. See you in the morning," Katie said, heading to her room to check her phone messages.

Turning on the speaker to listen to her new messages, Katie heard Chad's sweet voice telling her he made it home, and then the other three were from her kids, who were checking on her well-being from her episode only a few days prior.

Pulling her hair up and washing the makeup off her face, Katie put on shorts and a tank top for her four-mile jog.

"Bye, Katie!" Rachel and Casey said as they shut her front door.

The front door slammed. Feeling dizzy, Katie fell to her knees. She saw a man in his early thirties with dirty, black hair and crooked teeth. The man, who would be a single father of four sons, would be shot by his girlfriend with a rifle several times. The kids all witnessed. The woman would spend the rest of her days behind bars without remorse at all. Her kids then would be handed over to the state, separated by different foster families.

With their mom in prison the rest of her life, her children would have to grasp losing their father over $68.

A woman with no mean side to her, Katie couldn't imagine what would happen to the four boys left without their parents' support. A family torn apart by rage, the kids, who were all grown, would all go to prison for various crimes, getting lost in the prison system, only to come out ahead with a college degree.

Hearing her phone ring, Katie kept trying to focus on the name from the person calling. Seeing Chad's blurry name, Katie decided not to answer, knowing she would worry him just by the sound of her voice. Getting over to get a drink and calm herself down, Katie decided a nice dinner and shower would fulfill her plans for the night.

After her shower, Katie called Chad back, trying to sound as if nothing happened only an hour before.

"Hey, Chad. Sorry I missed your call earlier. My day just calmed down enough to call you back. I'm glad you made it home safely," Katie said, not in her upbeat personality.

"Katie, did it happen again?" he said, knowing that had to be the problem.

"Yes, some episodes are scarier than others, but the one today still has me a little shaken," Katie said, knowing she didn't want to burden him with her issues.

"I'm sorry for this happening to you, Katie. I wish there were something I could do to help you," he said, wishing he would've stayed another night.

"I will be fine, really. Hey. Guess what?" Katie said.

"What? You're taking the rest of the week off to come see me work?" Chad said, wishing it were that easy.

"No, Rachel is pregnant!" Katie said, trying to change the subject.

"That's great for her and her family!" Chad said.

"Friday isn't that far away. I'm looking forward to seeing you again," Katie said, sounding like a teenager again.

"Same here, beautiful. I'm heading to bed. Sweet dreams," Chad said, telling her good-bye.

Putting her phone down, Katie felt all alone once again, knowing she prayed for peace and quiet for so many years. Crawling into bed, Katie felt as if her appetite had disappeared. Falling asleep, Katie had nightmares all night about the images she saw only hours before. She tossed and turned and woke up sweating several times. *This has to go away before I lose my mind*, she thought, getting up to splash cold water on her face. Seeing her reflection in the mirror, Katie could see many new wrinkles under her eyes. With bags big enough to carry her to Italy, Katie decided to do the right thing. Katie decided to call her doctor for advice. Calling the exchange, Katie received a call only twenty minutes later. Telling her doctor about all her episodes, he advised her to go to the nearest hospital for a CAT scan of her brain.

"I can't. I have to work in a few hours. I just need some guidance from you," Katie said, hoping he would have the answers she wanted to hear.

"Katie, I can't make you get help. You have to make some sacrifices too," he said, sounding half asleep. "I thought they were only temporary, but they are getting worse and happening more often. I'm afraid it could be something far more serious."

"Okay. I will call my sister for a ride. Can you call ahead so they can do my test pretty quick?" Katie said, knowing it was 2:30 a.m.

"Yes, I will call right after we hang up. Please don't wait; go straight there," he said, hanging up the phone.

Walking into the emergency room, Katie was nervous as she informed the nurse why she was there. Quickly getting her processed, Katie went into a big room with only a bed and TV. Scared, Katie was wheeled right to her CT scan to make sure everything was okay with her brain. Looking around her empty room, Katie began to get cold as her nerves got worse. Unsure of the outcome, Katie saw a team of doctors come in and ease her mind that it was still just temporary.

"Ms. Roth, we have reviewed all the results and want you to know there is counseling and medications for you to take to ease some of your anxiety."

As her legs shook, Katie couldn't stay strong any longer as she started to cry. A young female doctor on the team handed Katie some tissues and reassured her that everything would be all right.

"Katie, we called your doctor and let him know the results already. He wants me to have you call his office for an appointment first thing in the morning, okay?" she said, sitting next to her on her bed.

"An important thing to remember is when you feel one of these episodes coming on, try to set your mind to good things that you have in your life. It's kind of like fighting a demon inside of your soul. It can be beaten. Please don't give up hope." the young man said as he shook Katie's hand.

"Thanks. I will be taking some weekends off for a while," Katie said, smiling.

Leaving the hospital, Katie called Chad. Looking at the time, Katie knew he would be awake. Telling him about her hospital stay and what they said, Chad was relieved it wasn't life threatening. Thanks for helping me out," Katie said, pulling into her driveway.

"Anytime. I'll text you later. Have a great day, beautiful," Chad said, putting a smile on her face.

"Thanks, you too!" Katie said, hanging up her phone. *Six o'clock; wow, what a night!* she thought, heading upstairs to relax. Dozing off, Katie heard her sisters come in the front door.

"Good morning, Katie. Are you awake?" Casey said, surprised she hadn't been to the kitchen yet. Jumping out of bed, Katie threw herself together and headed downstairs.

"No worries. Your studio is ready for the day," Casey said, worried by the look on Katie's face.

"Thanks. I had a rough night," Katie said, telling them what had happened.

"I saw you called in the middle of the night. I just thought it was by accident," Casey said, now feeling guilty.

Explaining to them what the doctors had told her, Rachel and Casey felt more relieved.

"Just takes time, I'm sure. I would say this is your challenge in life, but you have had more challenges in one lifetime than most people ever see," Rachel said.

"So are you and Ted excited about the baby?" Katie said, unsure of her answer.

"Yes, we are surprised. Chris is now sixteen," Rachel said, finding it hard to believe she was starting all over again.

"We need a baby around; ours are all grown," Katie said, knowing she still wasn't ready to be a grandma yet.

"It's meant to happen; God is blessing me with more," Rachel said, grabbing her bagel.

"Have a good day at work. This is Wednesday already," Katie said to Rachel as she went upstairs to her office in the library. "I'll see you this afternoon. The day should go by fast!"

"Good morning. Oh my, Katie, have you had any sleep?" Sheri said.

"No, I didn't sleep well. I only scheduled five models today because there wasn't as many applicants for the state of Georgia this time around, so hopefully my day will end by two o'clock," Katie said, heading downstairs.

Turning some music on to get herself in the mood, Katie changed back her studio to how she used to, but seeing Chad's idea made her wish it were Friday already.

"On our way, Katie!" Mark said over her cell phone.

"Thanks, Mark. See you in a few minutes!" Katie said.

With only a few select models, Katie's day flew by. Done before lunch, Sheri fed them before their flight out. Watching them leave, Katie thanked Sheri and went straight to bed for a much-needed nap.

Katie awoke to Rachel shaking her awake.

"Hey, Katie. We are leaving for the day. You should probably get up and clean up your studio for tomorrow," Rachel said, knowing her sister had been through a lot.

Hearing her cell phone go off, Katie thanked Rachel and answered her phone.

"Hello?" Katie said, still not fully awake.

"Hey, Mom. It's Ashley. Do you want me to bring you dinner? I'm moving next week to Devon's house," Ashley said.

"Sure, honey. That would be wonderful," Katie said climbing out of bed.

Heading to the shower, Katie felt a lot better already. Going down the studio to get ready for the next day, Katie heard Ashley come in the front door.

"Mom, I'm here." Ashley said.

"Okay. I'm downstairs," Katie said. "The food is in the kitchen."

"That's where I'll be; I'm starving!" Ashley said.

Finishing up in her studio, Katie was excited to visit with her daughter, knowing she wouldn't be seeing her as much.

"Thanks for dinner, Ashley. You know it's not going to be the same without you, right?" Katie said, hugging her.

"I know. I'm following my dreams!" Ashley said, excited about living in California.

Enjoying their dinner, Katie called Chad back, putting his mind at ease.

With the rest of the week flying by, Katie headed to California to see Chad only a couple of days later. Landing at his house, Katie was relieved to see him again, even though he had only been gone a few days. Hugging each other, Katie and Chad just relaxed for the two days she was able to spend with him.

Heading back home, Katie had to start training for her trip to Italy. Adding to her jogging, Katie decided to cut out any junk food and do more yoga and Pilates. With her workload slowing down a bit, Katie could already tell a difference in her sleep pattern.

"Good morning!" Katie heard from downstairs. Looking at the clock, it was only 6:00 on a Tuesday morning.

Nervous, Katie grabbed her robe to see who was in her house.

"Who's here?" Katie said, tiptoeing down the spiral staircase.

"Katie, it's just me. Relax," Casey said.

"Why are you here this early?" Katie asked, trying to catch her breath.

"Because I'm training Sheri in the library so I can run the studio next week when you leave for Italy," her sister said.

"Oh yeah. Sorry. I forgot about that," Katie said, heading back upstairs to get ready for her day.

Excited about her trip, Katie shut her bedroom door, knowing Casey and Sheri would be up soon to start their day. Numb, Katie could feel another episode coming on. Seeing an image of a teenage boy handcuffed behind a cop car, Katie was starting to shake.

"Katie, can I come in?" Casey said, knowing Sheri was never given the tour of the upstairs.

"Yeah, I'm heading to the bathroom to wash my face. Feel free to show her around," Katie said, splashing cold water on her face.

Convinced her episodes were there to stay, Katie called Chad to hear his reassuring voice.

"Hey, Katie. I took the next couple days off work. If you want me to come up to Missouri to see you before you leave for two weeks, just say the word," he said, always putting a smile on her face.

"Yes, I would love that!" Katie said, grabbing her clothes for the day.

Knowing it was her day off, Katie went for a morning jog and waited for Chad's jet to arrive. Getting his phone call, Katie drove to pick him up. Giving him a long hug and kiss hello, Cody gave them both a thumbs-up as they drove away.

"So any plans for us?" Chad asked.

"I don't know. I'm full of surprises!" Katie said, winking at him.